THE
LEGEND
OF SOCKET GREENY

Books by Tony Bertauski

THE

LEGEND

OF SOCKET GREENY

TONY BERTAUSKI

Dedicated to truth.

I

Life won't take you where you want to be;
It will take you where you're needed.
Like it or not.
Pike

To love deeply is to risk grandly.
One cannot be without the other.
Chute

Those who know, don't tell.
And those who tell, don't know.
Buddhist proverb

CHILD'S PLAY

Dreams rarely came to me when I slept. Visions were a different story. I could see them and feel them. Smell them. They were a glimpse of things to come.

This night while I slept, I saw a man walking down a crowded sidewalk, a man that hadn't seen daylight in years. A man destined to never see it again. But in the vision he was there, walking among people with the sun on his face. I wouldn't believe such a story anymore than Jack climbing a beanstalk. But this was a vision.

My visions were rarely wrong.

I sat up in a massive chair, my forehead numb from the desk, but it was nothing compared to the cold tingling sensation in my neck, a side-effect of visions, a dense uncomfortable numbness that took hours to fade. I rubbed my neck.

I rarely made it to bed. My desk served as a poor substitute. My office was oversized, to say the least. A hundred feet long, maybe fifty wide. The walls, floor and ceiling were made from microscopic nanomechs the size of skin cells and equipped to mold any object, create any environment or situation. It was also buried under a billion tons of granite beneath Garrison Mountain, home of the Paladin Nation.

Currently, the room was glowing blue from the intricate web of lines that represented naturally-occurring wormholes throughout the universe. It was the soft glow and pulsating stars that made me drowsy, but now I was awake with the image of a free man branded on my brain. A man that, given me the choice, would no longer be breathing. No going back to sleep now.

[Off,] I thought to the room.

The blue threads and twinkling stars disappeared, leaving me alone in the darkness. I called for the room to connect me with the man in my vision.

The walls bled brown from beneath the surface. I walked around the desk. The ceiling turned a deep shade of violet and a chair grew from a blackened floor. It was solid with stout armrests, immovable and empty. I paced to the end of the room with my hands locked behind my back and stared at the blank wall. The vision remained sharp and detailed, like a lighthouse illuminating deadly shores. And the dull sensation hung over my neck like a blanket of chains.

"Can't sleep?" a voice sang.

The chair was now occupied with a frail, bald man. His glasses were black, meant only to cover the white sightless eyes beneath, for the benefit of others.

"You should try warm milk," he said. "Dip some cookies in it, the ones with the creamy filling. They'll hit your stomach like a bomb, blow you into the next morning." He folded his legs. "At least, that's what they tell me."

Three hairless men appeared behind the chair, wearing black glasses. They were blind minders, as well, seeing with psychic vision instead of eyes, but they were no friends of the one in the chair. They stared at the man now pretending to dip cookies into a glass on his lap.

"You're dismissed." I waved at the three minders. "This exchange will be private."

4

The one in the middle said, "Request denied. Pike is to be kept under continual surveillance."

Constant surveillance? Pike was hardly a threat. After years of imprisonment and minder pressure, the fabric of his mind had been stretched and frayed, his thoughts and motivations splayed open like a butchered pig. His brain struggled to function and what few thoughts he had were hardly coherent. There was no need for three minders to contain his mind, hardly a need for one.

But he'd fooled us all before.

They resumed their focus on the man now double dipping imaginary cookies, shoving them in his mouth. "Uu unt sum?"

"At least back up," I said. "Give us some space."

The minders considered my request. Ignored it. Pike cowered under the intensified psychic heat that restricted the expansion of his mind. He looked over his shoulder like he just got slapped with a ruler.

"I call them Mo, Larry and Curly, you know. Larry's on the left and Mo's in the middle because he's the boss. And that's Curly there." Right shoulder. "I used to call him Shemp because he's not funny." A very serious look stretched over his face. "But Curly's my favorite. So, you know."

His favorite episode was *The Three Stooges Meet Frankenstein*. I knew that because he told me. And now he was going through it, scene by scene, and quickly seemed oblivious to me, as if telling the story to himself.

I walked closer to Pike's image and began to sit slowly, allowing the room to form a chair below me. It was wider than the one that confined Pike. I sat forward, resting my chin on my knuckles, allowing my mind to surround and penetrate Pike's mind. Even though he was just an image in front of me, something constructed by the room, it was projecting his presence from a secure location. It was no different than if he was sitting right there in front of me, laughing about the way Mo hammered Larry and Curly. His essence still flowed through the image, much like a voice travels through a phone. I could follow it with my mind, all the way back to the prison cell he shared with a rotation of minder guards.

Is there something the minders aren't seeing? It would be impossible for him to hide anything, but he'd done it before. He couldn't escape one of these minders. And three? Impossible.

I needed to see for myself, just to see if there was something they were missing. While he ranted about Mo's comic genius, I penetrated his mind like vapor. His thoughts were so disjointed, randomly appearing in a mix of memories and delusions, separated by basic impulses of hunger and sleep, that if he could escape he wouldn't know what to do in the free world.

His energy was jagged and broken, no longer the cohesive mindfield that he once was, no longer resembling the treacherous mind he used to deceive the Paladin Nation. A mind that could kill with a thought or hide secrets of betrayal. A mind that once tried to kill me. In his prime, it took a dozen minders to contain him. Now, he drooled on himself. But predators often lure their victims with deceit. *Good traps never look like traps.*

"What are you looking for?" Pike asked.

He caught me peeking, distracted by my own thoughts.

"No need to search far and wide for my thoughts. No need to be sneaky, it's open season on Pike, everyone's taking a turn. Why shouldn't you?" He pointed to the crown of his head. "You can look, but I'm afraid you're a little late, the cupboards are bare."

There were no dark corners left in Pike. No thought left unearth and analyzed. I retracted my mind and sat back.

"Don't like what you see, then? You're all powerful, the next coming of the world's savior. Right? Right? What are you doing, wonderboy, looking inside old Pike? Do you think there's a single thought these savages haven't raped? There's something left of me? I assure you there is not. I'm sure you already knew that." He turned his head slightly, awareness returning sharply, not so childlike. "So what are you looking for, wonderboy? Really."

"Tell me something," I said, "why did you betray the Paladin Nation?"

"*Booooring.*" He rattled off a long raspberry. "Whatever your real inquiry is, just look inside again, will you? Take a peek and see why I despise humanity. Go on, wonderboy, have a look. Have-have a look, won't you?" He punched the side of his head. "HAVE A GODDAMN LOOK!"

Spittle drooled over his lower lip. He leaned forward and the heat of the minders filled the room. Pike was yanked back into the chair by invisible restraints. His chest heaved, laughter gurgled in his throat, coming out in short bursts. He threw his mouth open, laughing silently.

To see a mind unravel was dreadful, but Pike was not worthy of pity. He betrayed humanity, tried to sell us to the artificially intelligent race of duplicated humans. He betrayed all those that trusted him and almost destroyed us. And for that, his mind deserved to be unwound and dissected. For that, he could not be allowed to go free.

The vision returned to me; the lighthouse swinging its beam around, projecting the details for all minds to see. I clamped my mind down, snuffed it out but not before Pike caught a glimpse.

He took a sharp breath. "You had a vision? Oh, you are a bad boy. A bad-bad boy, wonderboy. A bad, wonder boy you are, coming here to tell old Pike about a vision. The bosses are going to be pissed that you came here, yes they are."

Sloppy work, Socket.

"You had a vision about old Pike, didn't you, wonderboy. Didn't you? Oh, yes, I believe, I believe you did. You did, you saw me and you come here to see what old Pike would think about it." He twisted around and winked at Larry, then Curly, gave Mo the okie-dokie. "He had a vision about me, boys, you hear that? Good old Pike, gone but not forgotten."

Pike's location was undisclosed. Only a few knew where he was imprisoned. He could be in a cell a thousand feet below ground, or in a satellite circling the planet. With constant minder presence creating psychic static, I couldn't ascertain his location but, whatever the circumstances, no one could escape the Paladin Nation. Not even Pike on his best day. Still, I needed to know... *is he hiding anything*?

Pike bounced in the chair. "Let's play a game. A game, a game. A guessing game, what'd you say, wonderboy? A game, shall we?"

He looked at the ceiling, thinking hard, really trying to find the answer floating somewhere above him. Would it matter if I told him? No vision was guaranteed, there were so many variables.

"You saw something in the future," Pike said, "about me, I think. Do I get fat, is that it? I hardly get exercise in this chair. I complained to the warden but no one listens to old Pike, say that's what you get for betraying your species, or something like that, I don't know. Or I get relocated again, to another cell. You know, I like this one. I think it's the color. Brown just works. They turned it pink once and I didn't like that one bit, wonderboy. I started shitting myself and Mo don't like cleaning grown man underwear so they changed it back. You don't mess with old Pike's cell— Wait, I know." His smile was wide, the gums bright red. "*I kill your girlfriend.*"

He projected a thought and had I not been open and looking through his mind while he rambled, it never would've reached me. His thought was harmless, but clear to see. It was Chute, her sweaty hair stuck to her forehead. Pike had a knife to her neck. I squashed the thought.

Pike drummed his fingers across his pouting lip. "It'll hurt when I kill her, wonderboy. It'll hurt-hurt pretty bad, I think. And just imagine how your heart will feel after I strangle her, you know. How I lean over and suck the last breath from her lips." He inhaled, deeply, and closed his eyes. "It'll probably taste like cherry lip gloss. Your hearts will hhhhrr... it'll hurrrr...." He licked his lips. The smile died. "Hurt forever. Wonderboy."

I punched out with telekinetic force and his image rippled in the gale force of raw energy as it travelled through the image and found his body somewhere in the universe. I slid my mind inside him like a cold shank. He clenched his teeth like 120 volts shot up his ass.

"HOOO! What a grip!" He shook his head like a wet dog. Pain was better than nothing at all. "But tell me something, won-wonderboy? How am I going to kill your girlfriend if I'm in here —" He covered his mouth with both hands. Held his breath. "Don't tell me…"

I only blinked, but it was enough. He saw more of the vision than I thought. He was fucking with me.

"Are you joking? You're here to tell me…" He was bouncing again. "That I'm going to… escape?" He sang the last word like a little girl, the last syllable squeaky. "*ESCAPE?*"

I didn't budge, move or think. I wouldn't give him the satisfaction of seeing the details, wouldn't let him see more of the vision that revealed him wearing street clothes and smiling at the sun. I didn't want him to see that no one paid attention to the curious man until they got near him and his dangerous mind; how he projected a mere thought to tear a little girl from her parents. How he shoved her into traffic. Tires screeched. Someone screamed.

"Tell me, how do I do it?" he asked. "Oh, please. Tell me."

"It won't happen, Pike."

"You saw it, huh? Show me, right? Show me how it happens." He clapped his hands. "Please, pretty p-p-pleeeeeeease. I got to know, I just got to know."

I stood. The chair collapsed into the floor. "I'll alert the Commander of what I've seen. I promise, you'll not escape."

"Yes, but you could tell me just one thing?" He looked around the ceiling, again, entertaining the possibilities. "Do you know about *wheeeen* it might happen? I mean, I'm not saying it *wiiiiill*, but just in case. You know, I need to clear my calendar."

"Be advised." I projected the vision to the minders. Mo nodded. *Received.*

"Do I kill you, wonderboy? When I get out, do I kill you? That's not too much to ask, is it?"

"As long as I live, you will not walk free."

"Perhaps you should ask good master Pivot about that." He cocked his head. "Or is he still AWOL?"

Pivot. The greatest Paladin to ever live. My personal mentor. One that could see the future. One that disappeared over a year ago. I could still sense his presence, some days it was stronger than others. He was always around. I could feel him watching. I never thought much about the fact that he never showed himself, just secure that he hadn't disappeared entirely.

"Good old papa Pivot doesn't talk much these days, would you say?" Pike said. "Tell me, what's it like to be abandoned by someone you love? I'll bet it stings, like maybe it was your fault." He leaned forward and sniffed. "Maybe it's, you know... you."

"He's around."

"He is?" He looked in both directions. "Is he in the room right now? This second? Like an imaginary friend?" His laughter was high-pitched and much too loud. Cut right through me. "Poor wonderboy. All alone in the world. That's why he comes to see good ole Pike, he does. Lonely." He tipped his head back to the minders. "That's why he's here boys."

"You're broken, Pike. You deserve worse."

"Do you trust him, wonderboy? Do you trust papa Pivot?"

"He's the reason you're here."

"Yes, well all good things come to a screeching halt, they say. Just ask your vision, wonderboy." His tongue pushed through a smile. "Listen, you come to old Pike when you have your next vision." He dipped his head, let me glimpse the white eyeballs behind the black glasses. "I'm here to help, wonderboy."

He said it sincerely. He was a master of keeping an opponent off-balance. Nothing he said could be trusted.

The color faded from the walls. The images of the minders shrank. Pike melted into the floor. "Be sure to call my secretary," he said, his voice fading. "She can squeeze you in..."

I left the dark room, more disturbed than ever.

DISCARDS

I sat cross-legged in a field of manicured turf, breathing rhythmically in meditation. It had been weeks since the vision of Pike's escape and, still, it was with me. Most visions faded with time, but this one remained in full detail. Like a siren that refused to stop. I noticed my thoughts about it and returned to the present moment, listening to the birds sing.

Six kids sat cross-legged in front of me on firm, round pillows. Their eyes were closed and hands gently folded in front of their bellies. They tried to ignore the pain in their knees, sitting like concrete figures, holding steady, their breath coming and going. But they heard the birds. Dawn was near.

Sitting was almost over.

Their minds were in various states, some open, some scattered. The girls – Madeline, Aleshia and Grace – were mostly calm, but the boys were somewhere else. Joseph was dreaming, Dylan half-asleep and then there was Ben hating everything. His eyelids were cracked open, watching me.

They could leave the Garrison any time they wanted. But if they stayed, they had to commit to the daily schedule and that included food and a warm, dry place to sleep and a tropical forest. But there was also meditation practice, physical training and emotional therapy. The price for all these pleasures was but a gift itself: *Understanding*. I wanted to show them what they already possessed: essential wonder and unlimited freedom.

"I want you to return to this moment." I unfolded my legs, let the aches fade from my knees. "Allow the moment to be present. Allow space for your entire experience, whether it's excitement, resistance, love or hate. Allow space for whatever is in this very moment and be with it. Recognize thoughts about it. Notice if you want it to be different."

The dewy grass slid between my toes. I stepped quietly behind them, gently straightening their sagging backs.

"Just notice what you think and return to your bodily sensations. Allow the present moment to unfold."

Excitement vibrated around them. The best part of meditation was the end. They listened, remained sitting and present, but there was more exuberance than usual. Even Ben was grinning. They all cracked open their eyes, looking behind me.

The trees were far away, their canopies dense and dark. But even so, I could see the bright colored grimmets crawling along the branches, scurrying to get away without being seen. The little dragony creatures – no bigger than hummingbirds – were probably hovering behind me making faces or holding their tails up behind my head like horns to make the kids laugh. My frustration shot like sparks, rustling the leaves like a rogue gust of wind.

Grimmets.

They were psychic titans, each one of them with more mental strength than the entire human population. They defeated the duplicates, the entire population, several months ago without any hint of resurrection. I was the conduit for their power, for I understood. I saw life clearly. *The One Who Sees Clearly,* they called me. Through me, the grimmets called to all duplicated life forms on the planet, instructed them to deactivate and they did.

And now the grimmets were bored. And when the kids were around, they were insufferable.

"Socket?" Ben asked. "Ummm..."

Sigh. "Dismissed."

They jumped and ran, pulling at each other as they raced for the opposite end of the oval, grassy field. I let loose an ear-splitting whistle. They turned while running. I pointed at the meditation cushions tumbled in disarray. They fought, laughing along the way, and swept up the cushions to put them away. Every part of the schedule was their responsibility.

Ben fell down and rubbed his numb leg. Feeling came back slowly to his calf, and when it did, pins and needles tortured his nerves. "Why do we have to sit so damn long?"

No one gave Ben much of a chance. His father died when he was little and his mother was addicted to prescription drugs and mood-altering gear, anything that would make her feel good, escape the emptiness inside, until she mixed too many pills and never woke up. Ben landed in a children's home, like the rest of them, only he ran away. He was resistant, a fighter, but I saw something in him. And he trusted what I saw. That's all I asked.

When the pain ebbed, he hobbled after the others. They were already leaping onto the jetter discs nestled in the grass at the opposite end of the field that hovered off the ground once their feet locked in place. They scooped up sticks that were curved at the ends and flew across the field, the jetters tilting a few inches off the ground, responding to their thoughts for direction and speed.

The tagghet field was in the middle of the Preserve, a tropical jungle carved out of the mountain and protected from the elements by an invisible forcefield overhead. It was like a 5.2 square mile conservatory and the kids' very own playground. A place I thought of as home.

I walked to the edge of the field, where the trees met the turf, where a silver android awaited. His long plum-colored overcoat hung to his ankles. Colors flashed across his featureless faceplate, a bright red eyelight following the kids across the tagghet field. He held out a breakfast bar and a bottle of water.

"How was your morning meditation?" he asked.

I chewed the breakfast bar and observed the kids weaving expertly around each other. "Aleshia is ready to begin sitting every morning. I'd like to keep the others sitting twice a week, at least for another month."

"You should be aware that Grace is stealing food from the others."

Of course, Grace was stealing. I knew her memories, experienced them when we sat. Like the others, she was considered *damaged*. She ran from her memories, distracting herself with thoughts and desires and fears. Most normal people did that sort of thing, but no one could blame Grace. Her foster parents did unconscionable things to her. Mostly it was beatings, but some were sexual, the sorts of things that destroyed people, left gaping emotional holes that could never be filled.

But Grace was resilient. She had a lot of work to do. I wouldn't recommend meditation for a person like that, especially not that young. But she was different. All these kids were different. They didn't just endure; they were highly evolved, possessing an innate, genetic disposition for learning and transformation. I know, because I hand-picked them.

After the duplicates were defeated, the Paladin Nation needed direction. I launched the Orphan program. Ironic, I suppose, that the whole existence of the Paladins was to defeat an enemy that were like orphans. Duplicates had no maternal parents, considered themselves free and independent of the psychological problems that hampered humans. But the duplicates were programs, no matter how efficient they were, they could not *be,* could not transform and grow. Unlike the duplicates, the children could rise above their handicap.

I wanted to reach out to the human race, integrate the Paladin Nation into society, help people understand themselves. Understanding wasn't just a right of the Paladins, it was a human right. So why not start with society's most underprivileged. That didn't mean people would want the understanding we offered. Many people possessed a lot of psychological difficulties. Could they overcome them? We couldn't make them. So I selected the ones I sensed would.

"I would like Grace to join group therapy on Wednesday," I said. "I don't want to separate her from her peers, though. She needs additional support from some like-minded children with similar experiences. Empathy will go a long way for her. I'll be leading the group session. I also want to schedule Ben for individual counseling." I took a swallow of water. "I'll be leading that, too."

"But you are not approved to counsel the children, Master Socket."

They were on the other side of the field, but Ben spun around and looked at us, as if to make sure we were still there.

"He needs trust, Spindle. He trusts me."

"Do you have a suggestion on how to get permission?"

"Don't call it counseling. Just schedule him to chat with me for an hour. Let's start a week from now, on Friday."

"But you are leaving that morning."

The trip. I conveniently forgot. One of those things I was told I would be doing. All Paladins must make at least one trip through the intergalactic wormhole network. For the experience, I guess. My work was here, right now. I didn't need to see what sort of research was being done on planet Krypton or what alternative fuel was being mined from an asteroid.

Sorry, I'm busy, I wanted to say. But I already knew the Commander's answer. *No, you're not.*

Sunlight had crossed the sky, stretching long shadows over the field. Some of the grimmets emerged from hiding, fluttering over the kids, swarming so thickly they nearly buried them. Aleshia bounced the discus-shaped tag off the ground and the grimmets chased after it, then mauled Joseph when he snagged it with the magnetic curved end of his stick.

A red grimmet was in the trees behind me. *Rudder*. I could *see* all around me with my mind, feel the negative space between objects and *know* the essential spirit of all things, building an image of what things *looked* like in my mind. But I didn't need all that to see Rudder, he was different. I felt him, like a part of me that moved separately in the world. We had bonded when he brought me back from death and a part of me stayed with him. And part of him with me. He dropped onto my shoulder and wrapped his whip-like tail around my neck, purring.

[I told them not to do it,] he thought to me. *[I knew you'd be angry.]*

"I see. And you weren't with them?" I peered over at him, his golden eyes blinking. "That wasn't you, the red grimmet out front, sticking your tongue out to get the biggest laugh? That wasn't you?"

His eyes darted back and forth. A thought began to form in my head, in response to what I said, and then he shot off to join his pack in a chase for the tag.

"You need to do something about the grimmets, Spindle," I said. "They were very disruptive this morning."

"Me?" Spindle put his hand to his chest. "They will not listen to me, Master Socket. They only listen to you."

"Well, then, we're screwed."

The kids zoomed around the perimeter and came up our side. They held out their hands as they passed and I slapped them. Around the field they went again, a colorful cloud of grimmets nipping at their butts.

"Has my mother called?" I asked.

"She left a message that she will call in two days. She is very busy with Congress today and tomorrow." A smattering of dark colors blotted Spindle's faceplate. "The Commander is not pleased you met with Pike this morning without prior consent."

"I figured he wouldn't be thrilled."

"He would like to remind you that premonitory visions are to be immediately reported."

"He has a full report."

"He would like to emphasize *immediately*. He also forbids future meetings with Pike without his foreknowledge. The Commander is very reluctant—"

"I know how the Commander feels, Spindle. Trust me, there's no danger. Pike can no longer hurt me anymore than you."

Fact is, could anyone? I was the only telekinetic alive. I was almost seventeen, but I was not a child. I didn't like being treated like one.

The kids were coming around, again, this time with an empty jetter in tow. They pulled Spindle onto the field. The grimmets hovered over, cheering, casting a dark shadow over us, blotting out the rising sun. They helped shove Spindle on the empty jetter. Spindle's eyelight circled around his head. I nodded. He was off with the kids, tossing the tag back and forth.

I turned my back on the tagghet field to go inside Garrison Mountain, back to my office, wishing I had two lives. That way, I might make a difference.

JUST ANOTHER TOURIST

It was two days before I got back to the tagghet field. I was in the office the entire time, building mock scenarios, analyzing programs, having meetings by projection. My meals were brought to me and I'd experienced forty different countries through the office's magical transformations when, in reality, I never left the room.

The kids were begging me to come watch them; even Spindle suggested I take some time to come out, they were much improved. So I got outside and immediately felt the difference between fresh air and filtered air. Besides, the molding office had a certain taste, something that was fake and empty that penetrated every object and hung beneath every fragrance. I watched and clapped and slapped their hands as they showed off their best tagghet skills.

I took the long way back to the office, inside the mountain and down a wide hallway that curved left. Tall, rectangular windows were along the right spotting the floor with stretched boxes of sunlight on the floor. All of this stuff was new, an attempt to transform Garrison Mountain from a dreary tomb to something open and inviting.

I gazed at the wide boulder-field below that separated the mountain and the transportation wormhole on the far side, connecting our remote existence to the rest of the world. It used to be impossible terrain to cross, unless you had something that could hover. But now there was a road that dipped and curved through the giant rubble.

Girls in school uniforms, chattering in Japanese, came around the hallway bend. Their teachers tried to keep them together like shepherds. John Tackleton, their tour guide, was trying to keep up. He was a civilian, recruited a few months earlier to lead public tours through the Garrison.

Not only did the public have access to the Paladin facilities, they used the wormhole to transport back and forth from around the world. In fact, there were discussions about opening wormholes for public transportation, but that wasn't easy. To tear a hole in space-time required an enormous amount of psychic energy. Much of the Paladins' efforts went to just maintaining our own network. It would be decades before something could be done for the public. But the talks were in the works, and that had never even been considered before. Much like field trips.

The children ran to the windows, their shiny black hair bouncing. They ran around me like I was nothing more than a pillar. They pointed across the field and shouted about the wormhole. That was their favorite part of the trip, so far: one second they were in Tokyo and next they were here. And the weird feeling in their stomachs when they crossed over was like the world's tallest roller coaster ride that lasted all of a second. Wormhole transportation was never that fun, but we changed that, too. They said this in Japanese, but I understood. The words may be different, but thoughts and emotions were universal.

They ran for the steps and out of sight, on their way to the Preserve where they would forget all about the wormhole. The tour guide would tell them about all the great research the Paladin Nation was conducting in the Preserve and all the species of plants and animals it supported. Those kids wouldn't hear a thing once the grimmets arrived.

Word about the grimmets had spread across the world. The tours came to learn about the inner workings of the Paladin Nation, but it was the grimmets they came to see. Monkeys and otters couldn't compete with grimmets on their best day. In public, they'd already manufactured stuffed grimmets with wiry tails that kids hung from their book bags. They came in all different colors and people lined up to buy the newest release. *Collect them all!*

My footsteps dented the pliable floor of my office and the walls swirled with color, shifting and molding shapes from the floor and ceiling. A bed developed at my right and an entertainment center to the left. A large patio formed with folding doors thrown wide open. A cool, salty breeze blew inside.

My mother lay on the lounger on the balcony overlooking the Pacific Ocean. Her snores came in mild waves. I gently touched the railing. The resort was built right on the northern California cliffs, overhanging the tide that crashed on ship-eating rocks.

"Socket." Mother wiped the corner of her mouth. "I didn't know you'd arrived."

"Nice place."

She pushed her cropped hair behind her ear where it didn't stay. The same haircut she always had, but now with kinky strands of gray. She took a deep breath and stretched. "The view is fantastic."

We remained quiet, listening to the ocean speak. We did that often, just sit together without speaking.

"I see you're taking leave in a few days," she said.

"Chute's award ceremony." I looked over my shoulder. "She's Tagghet's Most Valuable Player, you know."

"Streeter going to be there?"

"He better be. Chute will skin him if he's not."

"I just thought with his new girlfriend, he might get… distracted."

Streeter found new love, a girl just as smart but twice as pretty. He should just propose now.

"You're coming back to the Garrison tomorrow?" I asked.

"No." She slowly got up and stood next to me at the railing. She was thousands of miles away, but I sensed her exhaustion as if she was right next to me. "California is aggressively pursuing a Paladin-sponsored education/conference center, but they need funding. It would be a great outreach for our integration program, but there's a lot of opposition from the government. Lots of suspicion."

"Who can blame them?"

"Yes, well, I need to convince them our policy of secrecy is a thing of the past and we're genuinely interested in sharing our knowledge."

"They're not buying it?"

"They haven't seen what we have to offer. Our advancements in health care alone will convince them." She drank from a water bottle and patted my hand. Her palm was warm and soft. "By the way, your Orphan program is doing quite well."

I hated that name, but the *Displaced Youth Program* wasn't catching on.

We talked about how many more kids we were planning to take on, how we could expand the program to the rest of the training facilities and, of course, get the word to the public on what a great job we were doing. I hated public relations, that was Mother's job. Everything we did, she had to find a way to tell the public. Television even started carrying the Paladin Network, a twenty-four hour news station that exclusively covered us. She was a weekly regular.

"I'm scheduled for my wormhole trip in about a week."

"Everyone does it," she said. "You nervous?"

"I'm not doing jumping-jacks." I drummed a short rhythm on the railing, watching waves crash below.

"I can't do anything to get you out of it, if that's what you're thinking," Mother said.

"No, that's not it at all. I'm just wondering why I need to go. Clearly there's a million things here I can be doing. I can't imagine why I'd ever be sent off-planet, so what's the point?"

"You sound nervous."

I glanced at her. She was serious. Then I realized, she was right. I was resisting some nervous tension inside me. Why was I being like this? It was just a trip, get it over with and be done with it and move on. Stop being a baby. But even acknowledging that feeling didn't make it go away.

"Look, I'm not nervous," I said, laughing nervously. "Okay, I'm nervous."

She laughed, too. I told her what I was feeling and she listened without responding. Maybe there was a good reason I was hesitant, I just didn't understand it yet. My gut feelings were often on the mark.

"I don't know." I spit over the railing and watched it disappear in the swirling wind. "Maybe it's as simple as not wanting to go through that wormhole."

"It's not comfortable."

"It feels like your spleen is getting squeezed out your ass, I'm told."

She grunted, pushed her short brown hair behind her ear. She'd never been off-planet, but she'd heard the stories. No one enjoyed the ride. No one.

A cruise ship moved from the left, the deck dotted with brightly dressed vacationers. I wondered if the party-goers were looking back at the shore.

"I read your report about the vision," she said. "About Pike."

"Not a happy ending, huh."

"What's your feeling? Does it have merit?"

I squeezed the railing. The quality of visions sometimes indicated their likelihood. When they were hazy, it was suspect, probably due to unforeseen variables. Even the weather could alter a vision, make someone stay at home instead of walk across the street and get hit by a truck. But when they were fully detailed, well, the odds were good.

"The vision was... solid." I swallowed hard. I hated to say that.

"Hmm." She nodded, thinking. "His security will be re-examined. Relocation may be considered."

"And maybe that's when he escapes."

The future was tricky. Perhaps if I never had the vision, he sits in his cell until the end of time. But then I have a vision and there's a relocation because of it and that's when he escapes. Self-fulfilling prophecy. It was much easier when I didn't know these things.

"Have you opened to related visions?" she asked. "Something that might clarify the event?"

Opening to visions meant trying to have one, but that never worked. They came on their own. I wasn't controlling them. But why did I have them at all? Was there some intelligent force deciding what to show me?

"There's nothing," I answered.

"Report any new visions, no matter how trivial." She watched the ship head for deeper waters, her thoughts coming in all directions.

"I better go."

"Yes." She took a deep breath. "I have a dinner meeting, tonight."

"A date?"

"No." She laughed. Anything personal like that was funny to her. "All business. Work never ends."

"It could, you know."

"And then what?"

Work was just a word, she once told me. What she did was her life. Why would she attend to anything else?

Her eyes were green. She looked at mine, like she often did. Like she couldn't believe how big her boy had gotten, as if she wanted to tell me to buckle my seat belt and make sure I looked both ways before I crossed the street. That mother-essence was strong in her, but sometimes it disappeared and she felt like a stranger staring at me, just an employee of the Paladin Nation, like she suddenly remembered something that chased the mother-essence away and I was all alone in this world. A stranger to everyone. Just like Pike said. Like he knew.

The ship was small on the horizon.

"I'll call when I get back from my trip," I said. "Tell you how they stuffed my spleen back inside me."

She smiled and patted my hand. Fatigue bunched in her shoulders, and then it faded. The details of the room washed away. I dropped my arms. The darkness of my office was cold. I hurried to the leaper, urged it to take me to the tagghet field where I could see real sunlight and breathe real air.

PINK SHIRTS

The days went by in a blur of commitments, but it still felt like my day off would never arrive. I was counting the minutes and there just always seemed to be more. But, finally, the week ended. Finally, I'd see Chute.

The parking garage was still a dank, stalactite-riddled cave. The dampness was in stark contrast to the rest of the Garrison, where the air was filtered and 85-degrees. A black car was waiting for me with the door open. I started to get in—

I hear rain battering the roof. In front of me there's an angry ocean, the waves white-capped and the water black in-between snaps of lightning.

"Everything all right?" Someone grabbed my elbow.

I was holding onto the car door. My entire body was quivering with the numbing sensation of a vision that normally only trickled down my neck. My gums felt dead; I tapped my teeth together to get the feeling back.

"Yeah," I said. "Just... I was, uh, just remembering something."

It took a second, then I recognized the someone that grabbed my elbow was a Paladin named Jaret. He helped me lean against the car. I sensed he was about to call for assistance, maybe bring a few servys down to check me out. I had enough strength and sense to convince him I was fine. I stood up, barely able to keep from swaying. He watched me get in the car. I waved him off.

"I'm fine," I said. "Training caught up to me. I didn't hydrate enough, that's all."

He waited, until I said, "No, seriously. I'm fine." I left with a glance back to make sure.

What the hell was that all about? A vision only a few days after that last one? And during the daytime with a full-body numb out? The details were so vivid. I felt transported to another space and time, like I was standing on a sandy beach. I should've reported it, but that was sure to screw up the whole evening. I'd do it when I got back. They could lock me up in the infirmary if they wanted. *Just not before tonight.*

"Are you ready?" The car spoke in a calm, feminine voice.

I took the wheel. "I'll drive."

"Very well. It is currently 60-degrees in Charleston, South Carolina. The wormhole transport is cleared for entry. After exiting, you are approximately thirty-four minutes from your destination. Please obey the laws and drive carefully."

An image of the boulder-field materialized on the dashboard. I eased the car over the slick floor and through the apparition of the cave wall into the field. The face of Garrison Mountain went up several hundred feet behind me, like a wall of resistance that the world needed to respect. It was the first thing tourists saw when they approached. It let them know we were big and strong. That they were safe.

I crossed the field and entered the dense trees on the other side to the swirling mass of the wormhole. I left Garrison Mountain behind. But the vision of the beach came along.

Cars were parked along side the road leading to the high school. Dozens of shuttles picked people up and carted them to the tagghet stadium. I continued down the road, people staring.

"There's no parking up there, dumbass," someone shouted.

Shuttle drivers directed me to turn around but I eased down the road until I reached the turnabout that looped in front of the massive high school steps leading to the front doors. I gave the car instructions to park somewhere far away; I'd call for it when I was ready. She said, "Certainly."

No one stared at me once I was out of the car. It wasn't like they couldn't see me. I wasn't invisible. It was a simple mind trick, that's all. I convinced people that the space I occupied was not interesting. They saw me. They just didn't care.

The car waited while I stared at my reflection in the window. My hair, still white, was long again, but not like a few years back. I'd gotten in the habit of pushing it straight back over my head, but it didn't stay there long, much like Mother's behind-the-ear habit. Most of all, I noticed what Chute called *the serious look*. My eyes were piercing; my jaw muscles flexed and my lips were a thin line.

"Smile a little," Chute would say, and squeeze my cheeks.

So I practiced in the driver side window. It looked like something from school pictures. Third grade. I tried again and it just got worse. "Go," I said, waving the car off.

I'll wing it.

I followed the crowd toward the tagghet stadium, one of the most expensive venues ever constructed at a high school, all funded by the Paladin Nation as an apology for the duplicates' deadly assault a few years earlier. The team went undefeated in the inaugural season, became nationally ranked, and had South Carolina's MVP. A girl with red hair.

The extravagant entrance was crowded. Little kids dipped their hands in the rectangular pond and high school teachers handed out brochures about the evening's events. A fox mascot tickled kids with oversized cushy hands.

The concession stand was inside the main gate selling popcorn and drinks and souvenirs to a packed crowd. Three girls passed by with green and tan shirts, *33 – 0* plastered on the front. On the back was Chute's face, a game photo of her holding her helmet with one hand and the curved tagghet stick in the other.

Most Valuable Player.

A vendor pushed through the crowd, holding up hats and towels. "You got any shirts?" I shouted.

He looked around, noticed I was standing right next to him. He reached in the box strapped over his shoulders. "I got three kinds, which one you want?" I nodded at the girls. "You want the girl shirt? All I got left are pink. You want the pink?"

"I'll take it."

He sold it to me and moved on. I pulled it over my head. Pink. No one saw me anyway.

I walked past the pedestrian ramp that led to the upper deck. The corridor was filled with displays hosted by student clubs and local charities. The awards night was as much for civic awareness as it was for jocks. I remained unnoticed until I saw the crowded display ahead.

It was the Student Virtualmode Club. They were future programmers that built elaborate virtual worlds and constructed complex gear to transport a person's mind out of their skin and into a sim where they could experience the Internet in virtualmode. Holographic monsters walked across the top of their banner. A hulking rock monster thumped its chest and an armored knight broke his sword over its head. The kids laughed, then watched a dragon waddle over and incinerate the rock monster.

The virtualmode students were talking to adults, explaining what the club did, extravagant membership fees and field trips. They touted the highest graduation rate among the student body and the highest grade point average. And scholarships, too. There were more scholarships available in virtualmode world building than any career field out there.

The bulk of the crowd was gathered in front of a short, plump kid explaining a gadget in his right hand. I leaned against the wall, near enough that I could hear what Streeter was saying.

"It will revolutionize the way we communicate," he said. "Our minds are as unique as our fingerprints. We can find anyone after we meet them by using this to capture their *mindprint.* You'll never lose track of family, friends or even pets. We can call them, link up with their mind, and then virtually *see* them as if they're in front of us. Virtually touch them. Space will become irrelevant."

"Not only that, once calibrated with your mind," Janette said, "it will record every thought and emotion you experience. It will record your *entire* life." Janette was by Streeter's side. She was short, too. "The government has already asked for a demonstration. He's flying to Washington next week. NASA wants to buy the rights."

Streeter looked at her and smiled. He may as well have batted his eyes.

"What do you mean *virtually* see them?" a dad asked.

"This gear," Streeter said, holding up the half-globe, "will link your mind with, say, your grandmother living in California. Your eyes will see her in front of you. You'll see what she's doing right this second, like she's in the room."

"Let's see it work," someone said.

"All right." Streeter scanned the crowd. Little kids raised their hands, jumping up and down, shouting *me, me, me.* He swung his finger around like a spinning wheel to pick the winners. He placed the gear against their foreheads, one at a time, and asked them to think of a friend or relative. And when they did, a holographic image of planet Earth materialized with a glowing dot on it, signifying where the person they were thinking of was located. And he was right, every time.

"Big deal," a kid said. "You said we'd see them."

Streeter smiled. "Oh, you're going to see them. I'm going to pick someone at random and dial up whoever that person thinks of?" He circled the spinning finger. "You ready? Huh? Who's going to be the lucky one?"

Me! Me, me, me!

The finger spun around. Parents were even raising their hands. The crowd grew larger. Streeter worked them like a street performer, waving his hand around and around. It started to come down to pick a winner—

> *Thunder rumbles through the sand under my feet. The next flash of lightning illuminates the silhouette of a figure in front of me. The heavy rain blurs the details, but I notice the knife in the right hand.*

"You there, in the pink shirt." Streeter was pointing at me. People were staring. "Yeah, you. I'm talking to you. Wake up. What'd you say?"

I was still leaning against the wall but couldn't feel my legs. I don't know how I managed to keep from sliding down to the ground. My entire head was ringing like a bell. I was moving my mouth but nothing was coming out. Now the kids watching the holographic battle turned around and looked.

"Hey there, stranger." Streeter came over. He laughed nervously, looked back at the crowd and pulled on my shirt. "That's a nice shirt. Isn't that a nice shirt, folks?"

They laughed nervously, too.

I managed a single step and it reverberated to the top of my skull. It hurt, but it brought me back, flushed away the heavy dullness.

"What's your name, stranger?" Streeter asked.

"Um. Socket."

"Boy, you nervous or just excited?" The crowd laughed, went along with the joke.

"Just, um, a little nervous, I guess."

"Nothing to be nervous about, my friend." He held up the gear. "Now I'm going to ask Socket to visualize someone in his family. That person is going to materialize in front of us. Now, normally, only Socket would see this person, but I've calibrated the gear to project it for all of us to see. But first," he put the gear in my hands, slightly heavier than a paperweight, "we need the locator to find Socket in time and space. Once it finds him, standing right here, it'll seek out his mystery guest."

Others joined the crowd to watch the pink shirt, funny-name kid holding a paperweight. All I could think about was the thunder and the lightning and the knife, how the figure felt familiar. And how I'd never had two visions in one day. Panic began to rise, along with a thought: *Not again.* Something was changing in me and I didn't understand it. Things like that made me nervous.

"Close your eyes, Socket," Streeter said. "Let the locator connect with your being, much like a virtualmode transporter pulls you from your skin."

I took a deep breath and relaxed. I was already feeling normal again. The last thing I wanted to do was freak a whole bunch of people out. I closed my eyes and gripped the locator tightly. I could feel it travelling through my arms like filaments, searching through my nerve lines for all my organs and the awareness of my being. It was a good prototype, but now I understood why Streeter chose me. It wasn't ready to fully connect with a normal person. He needed extra-perception, someone like me to assist its communication. So I fully engaged with the gear, letting it merge with my awareness.

"There we go," Streeter said.

I opened my eyes. A hologram of Earth materialized in front of us, turning on the axis, like it had done with the others.

"So the locator is finding Socket, it'll show us where he is, and then we'll ask him to…"

The crowd began laughing. A dot was glowing in the United States, but not in Charleston, South Carolina. It was in the middle of Illinois.

"You're only off by 800 hundred miles, kid," someone said.

Several people walked off, someone tossing in, "Good luck in Washington. Loser."

"No, just a second." Streeter took it from me. "I forgot to reset the... it'll still work..."

But he lost them. They were heading for their seats. The ceremony was going to begin in ten minutes anyway.

"Man, why'd you have to go and do that?" He scowled.

"I didn't do anything," I said.

"Because I made fun of your pink shirt?" He stared at it. "Why are you wearing a pink shirt?"

I showed him Chute's face on the back.

"They have those in other colors, you know."

"I didn't buy it for the color."

"Yeah, well, it doesn't work on you. And what's with the look of shock? You knew I was going to call you and then you looked like you were going to start drooling. You having a seizure?"

"Yeah, well, I just was... thinking of something. You caught me by surprise."

"More like I kicked you in the balls."

"Hi, Socket." Janette bobbed on her toes, holding Streeter's hand.

Janette and I talked while Streeter went over to the display. She liked my shirt and asked how I was doing and how excited she was for Chute. "Are you two going inside?" I asked.

"We got to break down the display," Streeter said. "And recalibrate this, apparently."

"You're close, Streeter. The code was correct and most of the internal structure. It must be holding some data from previous reads."

"We could take it back to the lab," Janette said, "run another test drive to realign the synapse relays."

"I suppose." He had that look again, as if she was speaking the language of love and only he could hear it. Then she blushed.

"I'm going to leave you two alone," I said.

"Well, come by later." He grabbed me before I could get away. "And don't tell Chute we're not in there. We'll watch it on relay, but I can't get in there to see it live."

"So you want me to lie?"

"No, just tell her you saw me and that I saw her, that's not a lie. If she gets suspicious, just run. That's what I do."

He looked at Janette for support, but she didn't know Chute all that well, yet. Chute wouldn't miss something like this for either of us and she expected the same in return.

"When are you bringing me out to the Garrison? You've had Chute out there like twelve times. Me? I've been there once." He put one finger in my face to make his point. "You like her better than me or something?"

"Infinitely."

"My feelings are hurt."

I pushed his hand away. "Every time I ask you to come out you got something planned." I stared at Janette for a long second. "Who's fault is that?"

She nodded in agreement. Streeter said, "All right, well, I got a life. Sue me."

"Maybe I could schedule you to come out in a few days, before I leave on a trip."

"Two days?" He rubbed his chin and glanced at Janette. "Yeaaaaah, I can't do that."

"You're hilarious, you know that?"

"How about this? I project into your office through virtualmode, you can show how the whole molding technology works. You don't need permission for that."

"I'll see."

Virtualmode club members grabbed Streeter and Janette followed. He pointed at me as if to say *do it.* I nodded but they were already discussing the next meeting, taking down the banner and boxing up the gear while the kids screamed for more action from the monsters. By the time I reached an entrance to the stadium, the corridor was mostly empty. Two minutes before the ceremony began.

RAINING ROSES

Eight-thousand seats in that stadium. All filled.

Lightners floated above the stadium spotlighting the crowd that cheered when their images appeared over the field in three-dimensional detail. Holographic fireworks streaked harmlessly from one side to the other, like a battle of green, blue and red fizzling missiles. Hundreds of shiny lookit orbs hovered around, their red eyelights circling their shiny softball-sized bodies, scanning and directing the crowd. I made my way near the front, stood along the railing just above the field.

Security guards were along the perimeter. There were some real important people on the stage in center field, including the governor, mayor and all the members of the county school board. The rest of the stage was occupied by coaches and parents. There in front, sitting with a blanket over his lap in a wheelchair, was Chute's father, Mr. Thomas, who was paralyzed in the car accident that took his wife's life. Behind him was Chute's older sister, Angela, her hands on his shoulders.

A bone-rattling explosion shook the seats, and then the sky lit up. Fog oozed from the tunnel at the end of the field, smoky tendrils crawling over the grass. Synthesized music hammered out a beat. The head coach emerged from the thick cloud and the crowd erupted.

He reached center stage and shook hands. And then the first player stepped from the smoke, hands in the air, dancing in a circle, whooping the crowd to another level of fanatical frenzy. Another tagger emerged, hopping up and down, swinging his arms. The announcer's voice barely registered above the excitement. The third player out broke rank and raced for the wall where fans leaned over with outstretched hands. The next one out followed until several of them were running along the perimeter shaking hands and signing shirts and programs. The crowd rushed down the aisles to get a piece of the action.

Two students pushed by me, booing. They threw poppers at the players, laughing with the squeal of gear-induced euphoria. Their energy tasted sulfuric, their synapses burning from the small patches they hid behind their ears that kept the dopamine production on high. They started to throw another round of poppers.

"Turn yourselves into security." I barely spoke above the noise, but they didn't need to hear the words. They felt them. "Report you are using illegal gear and need help."

Their complexions became pasty. They were frozen in mid-throw, absorbing what I just imprinted on their minds. They accepted my thoughts as their own, felt the compulsion to turn themselves over to the authorities. The command wouldn't last long, soon it would fade and they would resume control of their being, but it would last long enough to get them out of the way.

"AND, FINALLY!" the announcer shouted, "SOUTH CAROLINA'S MOST VALUABLE PLAYER..."

The crowd drowned his final word out, shouting a name that had been called hundreds of times during the tagghet season.

CHHHHUUUUUUUUUUUTTTTE!

38

Chute stepped out of the tunnel. My chest melted, seeing her step into the spotlight. The crowd began throwing stuff onto the field. My instinct was to stop them, but then I realized... roses. They were throwing roses. Some had stems, others threw just the flowers that perished in a flutter of petals that looked like a pink cloud falling onto the green grass. She raised her hands to catch them.

We would be together, for the rest of our lives, that much I knew because, from time to time, I had a vision. We're old. My hair is thin, but still white. Streeter is short, round and bald. Wrinkles soften Chute's face and her red hair is more of a rust color and sprayed with strands of gray. I'm holding her right hand. In her left, she holds a rose. We're in a wasteland of dead trees, their silvery-gray branches barren. Weeds brush against our knees until we reach an enormous stump worn and chiseled by the weather. Chute kneels and places the rose on the stump. We stand in silence. She lays her head on my shoulder.

It feels like we're paying tribute to someone, but I don't know who. All I know is that it's a solid vision. As solid as they get.

We'll be together, to the end.

Chute reached the steps leading up to the stage and the coach handed her a long stemmed rose. It was the students that started the rose ritual, throwing them like hockey fans threw hats on the ice after a hat trick. It started with any old flower, but when Chute was quoted on the news that roses were her favorite, it was roses the rest of the season. Whenever she scored, it rained red.

Her teammates pulled her onstage. Together, the whole team raised their arms. The crowd went berserk. It was several minutes before there was any control. In fact, no one could hear what the coach was saying. When he was finished, he turned it over to the other very special people. They handed out awards to various players. They each got to say something, shouting out to their friends and families and pretty much whatever came to mind. I could barely hear them.

Chute was the last up, blushing as the crowd ramped up again, tossing more roses, turning the field more red than green.

She held her father's hand and tried to speak but choked on her emotions, which only riled up the crowd more. When she finally spoke, and the crowd settled, she sincerely thanked everyone for coming, it meant so much. She held up the MVP award – a glittering globe – and the crowd responded.

"I hope this empowers girls everywhere. NOTHING IS IMPOSSIBLE!"

She wiped her face and kissed her father's cheek and hugged her sister. She thanked her mother and wished she could see her now.

Best ceremony ever.

It was almost midnight.

I waited at the back entrance, watching the team leave. Chute was the last out. She was escorted by a security guard to my car in front of the school. I opened her door, thanked the man and went around to my side and when I got in we met in the middle, hugging tight. I loved the way she smelled. "I knew you were there," she said. "It was like I could feel you, you know."

I know.

The last of the crowd was being ushered out of the parking lot by security. I took the wheel and drove down the empty road littered with programs and cups.

"Can you believe it?" Chute pounded the dash, shaking her head and screaming. "I'm going home with this! *Can you freaking believe it?*" She displayed the globe award on the tips of her fingers. The surface was clear and polished, but it was milky and opaque in the center, like it contained a galaxy. "Socket, I don't know if you know this." She eyeballed me, deadpan. "But I could be the best tagger of all time."

I laughed. "Where was that humility at the ceremony? I mean, all you did was thank everyone and hoped to inspire every girl to wear a sportsbra."

"Let's see if I go pro." She waved her hand around the globe. "Oh, mighty award that looks like a crystal ball, please tell me where I'll be in ten years."

Asking for the future made me cringe. I'd had enough of that. She chanted some mumbo-jumbo, fogged the glass with her breath and rubbed it on her shirt. She pressed it against her ear like a seashell.

"Socket! Guess what?"

"You win every tagghet award known to mankind?"

"No." She leaned close. "You're going to stop at a red light."

I eased up to the stoplight, already red. "Wow. That thing really does work."

"And now you're going to turn left."

"Um, your house is straight."

Her hand crawled across my chest. "But the park is that way."

"It's midnight, Chute."

"Oh my." She feigned surprise. "That means... we're going to turn into pumpkins any second. Promise me, Socket, they won't make me into a pie? Promise me!"

"But your dad is expecting us."

She nibbled on my earlobe, her breath in my ear. "I told him we were stopping at a party."

"He trusts me to get you home."

"Oh, you'll get me home."

The light turned green.

"Your dad," I said. "He has a baseball bat, you know."

"I just want to see the park," she whispered. "Is that so bad?"

"But you've seen the park."

Her tongue was hot. Shivers ran down my spine. "Not tonight."

The blinker flashed on the dashboard. I turned left.

PROOF

It was 12:50 when we got to Chute's neighborhood. She was looking in the mirror on the sun visor, fixing her hair. Her house was in a cul-de-sac, a single-story ranch with white siding. The lights were bright in the bay window to the right of the door. Her father was at the kitchen table. He looked up when my headlights flashed across the house. I turned the lights off.

"We're here."

"I look like I've been wrestling."

"It'd be good if you didn't."

"Give me a second, then."

"Your dad's watching."

"Let him watch. We're not doing anything."

Mr. Thomas sipped from a can, staring out the window. I tapped on the steering wheel, counting the seconds. Chute flipped the visor back. "All done. How do I look?"

The dashboard glow softly lit her face. Sometimes I forgot time when I looked at her. She was beautiful. Most would agree, but it was different for me. Her face moved me, deeply. Her smile. The way her eyes crinkled in the corners. Her energy swirled sweetly, vibrating somewhere inside me.

"What?" she said. "Do I still look like the Hulk?"

"No." I turned the car off. "Let's go in."

The doors slammed in the quiet night. We hooked our fingers as we walked up the concrete ramp. Chute pushed open the front door.

"There she is!" Mr. Thomas's voice boomed from inside the house. "There's my Annie-darling!"

Chute ran through the house. Her dad wheeled in from the kitchen. She kissed him on the cheek then walked behind him and wrapped her arms around his neck. Annie was her birth name, but her father was the only one that called her that.

"You letting the mosquitoes inside to breed, boy?" Mr. Thomas shouted. "Get in here and shut the door!"

I closed the door and came inside. Mr. Thomas held out his thick hand and shook mine and then Angela came running into the front room screaming. Chute laced her fingers with her sister and they both screeched. Mr. Thomas covered his ears muttering, "Jesus Christ's holy shit," and went to the kitchen for another beer. Can, not bottle. Mr. Thomas always said bottles were for girls.

The girls embraced, still screaming like ten year olds, bouncing up and down. He took a swig of Budweiser and watched his daughters celebrate. He flinched when they hit the high notes, but it never wiped the smile off his face. Angela was a cheerleader in high school, doing one of her old cheers, kicking her leg up high and shaking her hands. "A-W-E-S-O-M-E! Awesome. Awesome. To-tally!"

Chute imitated her, but was laughing too hard to keep up. Mr. Thomas's laugh boomed over the top of them. "You see that, Socket? They're taunting me with their perfectly working legs."

"Oh, stop it, Daddy," Angela said, not breaking stride.

Mr. Thomas put his beer on the table and wheeled over to the girls. He expertly leaned back and pulled a wheelie, moving in time to the dance. The girls kicked out like Russian dancers while

Mr. Thomas wheeled back and forth. The cheer broke down when the girls fell down laughing.

"Let's see that award, girl!" Mr. Thomas shouted.

The girls lay on the floor, catching their breath. Mr. Thomas waited at the table. The globe was by the front door, so I fetched it. He muttered thank you. And then the energy changed.

He gazed into the globe like there was something inside, oblivious to the ruckus on the other side of the kitchen. His eyes glassed up. Mr. Thomas was not the type to get misty, but the water in his eyes reflected the kitchen light. He held the globe close to his nose. His breath was choppy.

Angela leaped up when she saw the award, leaned over her father, hands on his shoulders, looking into it much the same way. Chute sat next to them. Suddenly, the house was very still. Mr. Thomas's lips started to move, but they didn't say anything. Angela felt him quiver, hooked her arm around his neck.

"Mom would be so proud, Chute," she said.

Mr. Thomas took Chute's hand. She laid her head on his shoulder. Angela wrapped her arms around them. Their energy intermingled, merging with deep sweet hues, connecting at a very real, essential level. All barriers stripped away.

Angela nodded at me. I hesitated. Mr. Thomas cleared his throat. "Get over here, boy."

Chute held out her hand. I took it, joined them at the table, felt the family essence weave into my being, their hearts beating through my arm next to my own pulse. I was five the last time I felt something like that, just before my father died.

We gripped each other tightly, staring at the globe. But it wasn't the award we were looking at. We weren't admiring its beauty or fame. It was a symbol of Mr. Thomas's family, represented how grown up they were. There was a time he was convinced he would never live to see it, but there he was. There they all were, wrapped tightly at the table.

Chute was a young woman. And here was something to hold, something to prove it.

Something her mother would be proud of.

"Don't close the door!" Angela shouted. "Dad said he'd get his bat."

Chute fell back on her bed, arms out. "Listen to her," she said. "She used to sneak out of the house all the time, and now she's telling me when I can close my door."

"You sneak out all the time," I said.

She rolled on her side, buried her face in the pillow, said something about the greatest day of her life. She used to have posters of celebrities and bands on her wall. They were replaced by a shelf full of trophies. She'd have to clear some space for the globe.

The only thing that remained the same was the picture over her headboard of the three of us. We were on the curb in front of Streeter's house. It was our first day taking the school bus. We were seven, had our bookbags strapped on our shoulders. Chute was in the middle, arms around us.

"I can't sleep," she said into the pillow. "Will you stay the night?"

"Right."

"You can sleep on the couch."

"I told you your father had a bat. If he finds me on the couch in the morning, he'll use it."

She lifted her head. "You can hide, then knock on the door like you came over for breakfast."

She's serious. "Look, I'd love to see you all day and night, but I can't. Not tonight."

"The world can wait." *Still serious.*

"I've got some things to do, and there's a trip."

"Where are you going?"

I grabbed a tagghet puck from her dresser, inspected the scuff marks. "Somewhere far away, but it won't take long."

"Well, I guess I'll have to get used to you being on the road, once I'm Mrs. Greeny." Her laughter muffled into the pillow. "It's not easy being the wife of a superhero, you know."

46

"I'll bring you to the Preserve when I get back. I've got some kids that would love you to teach them some tagghet moves."

"Really, really?"

"Promise, promise."

She rolled over, closed her eyes and hummed. Her sleepy imagination flashed with images of trees and grimmets. "Could you do that energy thing?" She tapped her forehead. "I'm not tired."

I sat on the bed and touched her forehead. My essence mingled with hers and our experiences merged. A closeness. Oneness. Something that reminded us we were never alone.

She was softly snoring within a minute. I stopped at her doorway and glanced at the picture of the three of us again. It seemed like just the other day. I leaned closer. The details were smudged in the background, like there was a figure using back-reflecting gear to appear invisible. Then again, it could just be the printer smudging up.

I had a gut feeling that wasn't it.

TO REIGN

The roads were empty and slick from a light rain, reflecting the street lights. I turned the music off and cruised down the Interstate. I didn't miss leaving South Carolina, but I hated leaving Chute. Someday, I could bring her with me. But then what? Are we going to play house inside Garrison Mountain? I was still so torn about my two lives. Somehow they were going to merge. Maybe one day I could retire and find peace and quiet and a normal life when the world was saved.

I took my exit after crossing the Cooper River bridge, the blinker flashing—

> *The figure steps forward, reveals the strands of wet hair over her face. Red hair. Chute lifts the knife, her face twisted with anger. Then she leaps, swinging the weapon down at me, lightning flashing off its edge.*

"Auto-pilot engaged," the car reported.

49

The tires hit the gravel on the shoulder as the wheels turned the car back onto the pavement.

I was slumped in the seat. My lips were fat and rubbery. The moon passed between branches. The car found its way to the secure location of the wormhole while I tried to get the feeling back. Only when we entered the blue swirl could I take the wheel. I wasn't thinking clearly, but I knew enough that these weren't normal visions. If they got any stronger, I'd be dead. I had to get some answers.

I flew across the boulder-field toward the vertical wall of the Garrison. The Commander would get my reports soon enough, but not before I made one last stop. Call it compulsion or gut-instinct. Or insanity.

If I have anymore visions, Pike said. *As if he knew I would.*

I called ahead to my office. When I arrived, Pike waited with his legs folded beneath him. A string of spit jiggled from his mouth. The minders appeared behind him.

"Wha' dewyew wan?" Pike lifted his heavy head, his dark glasses askew, revealing the white eyeballs filled with rooty veins. "So soon?" He smacked his lips and sat up. "To what do I owe the pleasure of—"

"What do you know?"

"I know, I know… what do I know? What do *you* know?"

"You know something, Pike. Something about the things I'm seeing. You tell me WHAT YOU KNOW!"

His mind was scrambled, thoughts floating like weeds in the ocean. Perhaps that was the idea, make things chaotic, hide the secrets in plain sight. Like a shredded document thrown into the wind. It would take centuries to put it back together. And the minders just kept blowing.

"Play a game with me, wonderboy, shall we?" Pike smiled.

"You think this is a game, Pike? You've lost your mind."

"Quite right, you are. But if you want me to tell you things, ole Pike will tell you things. Let's play a game."

I snatched his neck; the knobby Adam's apple pumping up and down in my palm. "You tell what you're hiding, you filthy traitor. You know something about these... these *visions.*"

He slid his glasses back up his nose with a single finger and waggled his eyebrows. I threw him against the seat and paced to the back of the room. This just didn't make sense, these experiences were unlike any others, but now they were bringing images of nonsense. In what universe would Chute attack me?

I crossed my arms, staring at the back wall. Had I made a mistake coming here? No, Pike knew something. He was very specific about *if I had anymore visions.* He knew.

Eh-hem. He tapped his foot.

I looked over my shoulder. "This is all just a game to you."

"It wouldn't be any fun if it wasn't. Indulge me." He waved his arms and the floor shifted between us. A checkerboard formed with globular shapes, each taking a space. "And I'll tell you everything."

The globular shapes were black and white, each of equal number. Outwardly, each piece looked exactly the same, but each was as unique from each other as a dog is from a cat. Another checkerboard formed several inches above that one, this one smaller with fewer squares. And above that, another smaller one and another, until there was a total of seven boards forming a pyramid, the top level a single square at eye-level.

Reign. He wanted to play Reign, where the rules and moves were beyond the comprehension of ordinary people. The object: get the king piece to the top. First, one had to see the king piece, but not with your eyes. It required opening your mind, to see the pieces differently, to feel them, sense them with extrasensory perception.

I sat down in a chair forming below me.

"Ill-advised, Paladin Greeny." The middle minder stepped forth. "Opening your mind to a convicted—"

"THERE IS NO THREAT!" The walls shook. The minders felt the infinite power of my mind peel through their advanced minds. They faltered, then resumed their dutiful focus. My outrage would be reported to the Commander. Hell, I was surprised the room didn't just shut down. But it didn't.

Pike looked over his shoulder. "You're talking to wonderboy here, Mo. Better watch yo' self before you wreck yo' self." He threw his head back and howled.

What was becoming of me? I didn't like the mystery. Why did it seem the answer was right in front of me? It just countered any logic, but still, there was something here. I was losing control of the visions, why were they changing?

I scratched my chin and considered the multi-layered game and innocuous pieces. Pike waited patiently. And then I opened. He sat up, tasting the availability of my mind, its essence wafting toward him. His feeble mind crept forward like arthritic fingers. Pike clapped. *Pitter-patter.* "You-you go first, my guest. Guests go first."

I allowed my awareness to penetrate the game. The generic pieces exposed their true shapes as my psychic vision opened, forming rooks, animals, weapons and warriors. Pike's pieces flickered, changing identities as he integrated with them. This was a game of deception. Of hiding. And exposing. It required strategy and trickery, the ability to hide deception within deception within deception. To lay traps within traps.

Pike's mind entered my space. It was ragged and frayed, but still capable. It observed how I moved, how I planned. How I reacted. In turn, I reached out for his mind, to see what he was planning. Looking into your opponent's intentions was the equivalent of looking at one's cards in a game of poker. But Reign was psychic deception.

Sometimes you wanted them to look.

"I see, I see," he said. "You have dreams."

My pieces flickered back to ordinary shapes, away from the powerful warriors that defended my regal king piece. His gallant knight pieces crossed the bottom board to trap me.

"Not exactly dreams," I said.

"Who do you think gets the rose?"

"The what?" Pike's monkey-beast pieces advanced to the second board, pulling his king piece with it while his knights kept the majority of my pieces trapped. He was talking about the vision where Chute places the rose on the stump. "I'm not talking about that one."

"Because you like it, do you?"

"Because it makes sense! None of the others..." I stopped short. He didn't need to know anything else, but it left me wondering how he knew about the rose and the stump.

"Who says that is you?" His laughter was almost a growl. "In the vision, it looks like you, but who says that-that is you with her, huh?"

"What?"

"Your dream." He coughed. "You think that is you in your dream, in your vision. You... with your..." He coughed, again. "You think that's you with your wife?"

"Who else would it be?"

"Well-well, now. Looks can be a tangled web we weave, if we seek to deceive." He gazed back at the battle. "Or something like that."

My pieces transformed into nimble swordsmen slashing his pathetic soldiers into pieces before advancing to the second level. Only a strong ring of rooks formed around his king piece kept me from destroying everything.

"Who is sending these... vi-vi-visions to you?" he sang.

"No one *sends* them."

"Oh? So you, you think them up, huh? You think up the future, wonderboy? Is that how it works?"

"Insights are an extension of my being, a connection with presence. The moment contains all past, present and future."

"Oh, you are such a treat, wonderboy." He laid his head back savoring the moment like it was melting on his tongue, then spoke softly. "If they are an ex-extension of you, then why don't you stop them, huh?"

"They have something to show me."

"You? You have something to... to show you?"

My pieces transformed into brutes with oversized axes and began chopping at the protective rooks, bricks and mortar scattered across the second level, trickling to the bottom board. My king advanced to the third level while his cowered behind the crumbling walls.

"Don't patronize me."

"NOR ME, WONDERBOY. "

A force of a once-great minder punched the unguarded fabric of my mind, but it was mild, nothing more than a slap, and I took advantage of the distraction by wiping out the entire second level. His king piece leaped to the fourth level, but without protection it was doomed.

"*Who* is sending you visions is irrelevant." He looked over the game while his king drew a sword. "A better question is *why* he is sending them."

"Why is it a he?"

"He, she… whatever. God is a he, no? Yes?"

My three warrior pieces, the only remaining besides my king, surrounded his king piece. I would walk to victory.

He laughed *at* me. "Where is someone taking you, wonderboy, huh? Steering you like a ship to where, huh? That is the question you should investigate. That question you should be asking and answering. Wrong questions beget wrong answers."

My warrior pieces transformed into enormous serpents with impenetrable scales and dagger teeth. My king piece slowly moved up behind them.

"I control my own destiny. I am responsible for my own actions. Are you having difficulty accepting your own fate, Pike? *You* betrayed us. No one else is at fault for that."

"Don't lecture me." He spat on his lap. "I despise this flesh and everyone like it. You like it there in your skin, wonderboy?"

I took a moment to gather my composure. Pike was controlling the conversation. He could plant suggestions in a victim's mind with a seemingly innocent conversation. Great minds did not need to overwhelm victims to beat them. Victims of great minds never even know they're beat. They never even hear the swooshing of the guillotine; only feel the pinch of its blade.

Pike sang a song while my king piece climbed to the sixth level. "Why do you come to see me?" he asked, unconcerned he would lose.

"I come," I said, slowly, "because I cannot accept a world where you live."

"Oh, that." He raised a finger and cleared his throat. His king piece spiked the long sword, its only weapon, into the board, clearly giving up with no options past the vicious serpents. "I particularly enjoy that vision, wonderboy. It gives me reason to live, if you want to know the absolute truth. That one day, I may be free to murder and pillage and raze this planet, that-that-that gives me hope there is a god." He raised his arms up and gave thanks to the ceiling. "There must be a god, don't you think?"

"No god would allow you life."

"The world needs the devil."

"Love is the reason the world exists."

"And evil is its soul-mate."

"I could end you, Pike." He felt the power of my mind slither coldly inside him. With a thought, I could will his heart to stop. My king paused.

"That would be… suicide." He struggled to breathe. "Death to me… there-there would be no reason for you."

"It would be justice."

"Are you God?"

"No," I said. "I'm the judge and jury."

"Then I want a new trial."

I removed my mind from him. He only got pleasure from it, anyway. Any feeling was better than the numb imprisonment he endlessly experienced. I had all I needed from him. The game was over, there was no need to finish. Sometimes gut feelings led to dead-ends. The details of the room began to shrink as I got up.

"Have a safe trip," Pike said.

I stopped. The room remained in full detail. I recalled my last interaction with Pike, found no reason that he should know about the trip. When I turned, he smiled mischievously, like a child that sprang a secret.

"How do you know about that?" I penetrated his mind again, but there were only random thoughts. Pike offered no resistance to the invasion, relishing the uncomfortable sensations of his stretching mind. "Tell me, Pike. How do you know anything?"

"You think-think old Pike is useless, huh? There are things that… leak in the air, you know." He waved his hands like a magician pulling something from space. "Perhaps I know you better than you know you, wonderboy?"

You never even hear the swooshing of the guillotine.

"You know, it's funny," he said. "If you think about it, we don't control anything, really. The universe tosses us about like an ocean of water. Really, we're just driftwood. If you think about it, really. That-that-that's what I think."

"You're a plague."

"We remember pain, wonderboy. *Remember that.* Pain makes us feel *human.* Do you understand? It is not love that reminds us of who we are, it is pain, it is loss, *it is death.* Humans relish suffering, holding it close to their heart. They define themselves by the hurt, do you understand, wonderboy? Do you? We are vulnerable. Pain reminds us of that, that we exist. It is not love that we remember."

He lifted his chin, as if to offer his neck. Pike was repulsed by his own flesh, yet he craved the satisfaction of his being, his own essence. To feel. To be. He wanted to escape the misery of his ghostly existence, the separation of his own self, divided into psychotic elements. He did not see clearly. And for that, he would always suffer.

"Remembering is not a prerequisite to humanity," I said. "It is our presence."

"But it helps. Otherwise, you are a goldfish."

"Without presence, we are computers."

"Oooo, touché. Memories and presence. Like milk and cookies, would you say?"

His king had taken a knee with hands folded atop the jeweled hilt of the long sword. My king reached for the top square and the serpents opened their daggered mouths to devour his king. And as they bit down, as my king neared the top, a long steel tip slid from the top square through my king's head, impaling him moments from victory. Somehow, Pike's king stood victorious at the top, the serpents left squirming on the ground.

You only feel the pinch of its blade.

"You come with questions," he said. "I give you answers."

He was no longer smiling like the insane, but for once appeared quite lucid.

"You give me nothing."

We stared for several moments until a smile finally broke his face. I called the room to break the connection and flopped into my chair, no clearer than I was before this senseless meeting.

"If you see papa Pivot, pass along a message for me," Pike said, as the details of his image began to shrink. I heard him shout one last word from a long ways away, could feel him smiling when he said, "SHOWTIME!"

Perhaps the Commander was right. He was not one to toy with.

KNOTTED

My office was filled, once again, with the intricate web of wormholes that infiltrated the universe, illuminating the blank walls with an electric blue haze. It was a map to the universe's roadway system and I was supposed to know it by now. I sat with my feet propped on the desk.

I just couldn't concentrate. I couldn't ever remember how many hours had passed since I left Pike and that was the first time I could remember ever losing track of time. I always knew everything, down to the very second, like my mind was a ticking clock. Now I felt like some insomniac consumed with work.

Sound familiar?

Back in my old life, before I was aware of my Paladin-nature, I spent countless nights waiting for my mother to come home, only to answer her calls that something came up, she was stuck at work. Sometimes I'd stare at her image when she video-called, notice the dark rings under her eyes, wondering when the last time she'd slept. Now it was me.

It wasn't some trivial distraction that had me wide awake. I wasn't even thinking of the wormhole trip or the strange visions. It was Pike. The guy was a mental master and here I went and underestimated him. Even in his decrepit state, he knew how to hit me. He had me so consumed with him, I couldn't think straight. Or sleep.

He had answers to something, I could feel it. But I wasn't asking the right questions, that's what he wanted me to know. I think. Had he become some brat smirking behind his hand while he watched me step into an obvious trap, milking every second of joy from my immediate future? Am I walking into it? Is he leading me there? Is this part of it?

Get a hold of yourself!

I dropped my feet and rubbed at my tired face. I really needed sleep, this was no way to deal with problems. But I'd just end up staring at the ceiling. And I couldn't let this go. *If I'm going to obsess, may as well stop half-assing it.*

"Show me Pike," I said.

The maze of wormholes evaporated, leaving a wide open blank space between my desk and the opposite wall. An image flickered a few feet in front of me, then materialized into a solid projection of a figure slumped in a chair. This was simply a projection of what Pike was doing at that moment. He couldn't see me. Didn't know I was watching.

I paced around the desk. The three minders solidified in front of me, like immovable objects staring at the back of Pike's bald head. Pike was hunched over with his legs folded under him, swaying back and forth like a mental patient. The ever-present string of drool jiggled off his lip while he mumbled. His glasses had fallen off, lying in his lap, exposing the sightless eyeballs that were filled with red veins.

I knelt in front of him. This is how he spent his endless days. There was no sleep. No exercise. Just second after second of the minders frying his mind like a microwave.

Showtime. What'd he mean by that? Out of everything he said, that stuck with me, like he knew something was coming.

Something to do with Pivot. Or was he just clever enough to make me think he did, because there was no way this secluded madman could know anything.

I paced around the empty office, leisurely throwing each foot in front of the other while I stared at the black floor. It was dark at the far end, barely lit by the image of Pike muttering near my desk.

What makes you believe that's you?

The space brightened around me as I called up the vision. Weeds sprouted from the floor between rising boulders. The rose in Chute's wrinkled hand. I walked around to look into our faces. The traces of white hair, thinner and receding, covered most of my head. How could that not be me? But now he had me wondering. I looked back at the image of Pike, still wavering. Still mumbling.

That's me. End of story. My visions weren't wrong.

So does Pike escape?

I waved the image away just as Chute placed the rose on the enormous charred stump. I was standing in darkness again, hands clamped behind my back, no more at ease than I was ten minutes earlier. And Pike still chattering.

"See Chute."

Chute's bed materialized in front of me. It was a live feed from her bedroom. She let me tap into her home's security months ago. We started to project images back and forth like I did when I met my mother, but it was just too impermanent. We didn't use it much anymore because we decided if we were going to talk, it had to be in person. But sometimes, I would call it up just so I could watch her sleep.

Her head lay softly on the pillow, eyes shut. Her lower lip fluttered with each exhale. Sometimes I'd watch her long enough to hear her sleep talk, but there were never words, just moaning and turning.

I sat on the floor, wishing I could stroke her hair. All I could do was watch. It was better than nothing. At least I knew she was safe. I recalled the vision of her attacking me, more impossible than Pike escaping, even in the most bizarre alternate reality. She wasn't capable of that, not with me. Not with anyone.

So maybe my visions were going off the rails after all.

"Your visitation rights with Pike have been revoked." Spindle was standing by my desk, his red eyelight glowing in the dark. "The Commander has put a moratorium on your contact with him until further notice."

A lock of hair fell over Chute's face and was puffing out with each breath. I wanted to move it, all too aware Spindle was patiently waiting for me. I stood and turned my back, my steps shuffling a bit. Fatigue filled me like sand. I felt so heavy.

"I believe it would be prudent for you to get some rest, Master Socket."

I was nodding. He was right. I wanted to tell him I was heading to my bedroom, but stopped in front of Pike, mesmerized by his repeated movements.

"Why are you watching him?" Spindle asked. "He should not be of interest."

I was still nodding like I was stuck in a trance, transfixed by Pike's suffering. I could feel Spindle's eyelight on me. Finally, I muttered, "Because I don't if I can trust my visions."

"Are you referring to Pike as a free man?"

Pike jerked in his chair like he heard his name. His head rolled around and settled. "There's that," I said. I told him about the blackouts and the intensity of the visions that were nonsensical and unsettling.

"You have not reported these visions, Master Socket. The Commander will be displeased."

Pike was back into his moaning rhythm again.

"I'll report them," I said. "It's just… these visions are different. They keep drawing me back to him." I gestured to Pike. "Somehow, he knows I'm having them. Like he knows what they mean."

"That is impossible. He has no means of contact outside his confinement, and that is precisely why the Commander forbids you further contact."

"He knows something, Spindle." I looked directly at his eyelight. "I can feel it."

"Would you like me to schedule an appointment with the minder psychologist? Perhaps he can unblock subconscious thoughts that will allow you some understanding of your situation."

I looked across the room. Chute rolled over and settled back into sleep. Maybe he was right, I should get things checked out. Maybe someone could help me get some clarity. Or maybe, for once, my future was cloudy. I'd known about things that were about to happen for too long and now it was bothering me that I didn't. Maybe it would be good to be in the present moment without knowing the future.

I shook my head. Spindle's eyelight brightened. He waited for me to respond. I called for the room to kill the projections. Chute and Pike's images faded out and the walls began glowing to keep us out of the dark.

"Perhaps we should begin a review of your wormhole travel." Spindle took a step. "Your trip is in two days and you still have to complete the orientation."

"Tomorrow. Right now I need to sit."

"If I may suggest—"

I held up my hand. "Thank you, Spindle. But we can go over this later."

"Very well."

The office transformed into the darkened forest, a live feed from the middle of the Preserve. The floor sprouted the green turf of the tagghet field with trees all around. I went to a meditation cushion nestled in the lush grass. The sky was dark, but sunrise wasn't far off.

"Spindle." He stopped before exiting. "Send the kids up here when it's time for them to rise. We'll sit in my office this morning."

He nodded and left. I folded my legs and straightened my back, taking a deep breath. The present moment felt so fragile. I didn't like that, but being present had little to do with how I felt.

LOST IN SPACE

I stepped out of the shower room and pressed my face into a towel. It'd been over fifty hours. Still no sleep. I was feeling it in my face, but my eyes refused to shut. The exhaustion wore on me like a suit of armor. I wasn't fighting it anymore; I just let the heaviness be there. Still, no sleep.

I'd finished a long game of tagghet with the kids earlier that day, told them about Chute's visit when I returned. Playing tagghet with me and Spindle was one thing, but testing their skills against one of the best high school players would let them know where they were. The boys weren't half as excited as the girls until I showed them an image of her. She was talented *and* hot.

I got dressed and sat on the bench, leaned against the wall and closed my eyes. Maybe I could catch some sleep, but when I took the leaper to my office, it was filled with the electric blue lines of the wormhole network. Miniature galaxies were suspended throughout the web.

"This can wait no longer, Master Socket." Spindle was standing next to my desk. His tone was stern. His eyelight intensely glowing, lighting the surface of my desk like it was on fire. "Your launch is scheduled twenty hours from this moment. It is critical that you understand your journey."

He said it like he meant more than just the trip.

I stepped through a disc-shaped galaxy and put my hands up like the web had snagged me. "You caught me."

"If you kindly step next to me, I can begin."

"I'm joking, Spindle. Come on, you wake up on the wrong side of bed this morning?"

"I do not sleep, Master Socket."

"I know."

He didn't reply, simply waited until I stepped through the dazzling blue lines criss-crossing my path. I finished putting on my shirt. "You have my undivided attention."

"Thank you."

So Spindle started off with the history of wormhole development, how the Paladin Nation began space exploration before the Wright brothers were even born. It was information I already knew, but I wasn't about to interrupt. That eyelight was as bright as I'd ever seen it.

Natural wormholes existed in space. In fact, most planets were connected to one and once the Paladins learned to access the one flowing through Earth, they had access to the universal wormhole web. Paladins developed special equipment to travel through them and began mapping the universe. My office was filled with every known avenue that existed. If a traveler was skilled enough, he could jump from one galaxy to the next. Most Paladin space travelers never returned, spending their lives somewhere in the galaxy, jumping planet to planet, mapping and sending back their data as they went.

"Your ship will be programmed to take you to your destination," Spindle said. "But it is critical that you make a psychic connection with your ship for accurate projection. You will experience an instantaneous relocation to your destination. It is quite unpleasant."

"I know what a wormhole feels like."

"Traveling from the Garrison to Charleston is not the same as traversing the universe!" His words were sharp. "If you lose a psychic connection with the ship, you could lose your way, Master Socket. One errant thought and you could be lost in space."

His eyelight was reaching laser beam intensity. I nodded slowly.

"You need to be rested before you depart. You must be able to focus."

"Noted. I'll knock out a nap as soon as we're done."

His eyelight relaxed, dimming down to a subtle glow. He appeared to tower over me, examining my true intentions. Finally, he stepped into the web of wormholes, tracing one particular line with his finger that sparkled as he followed it into a massive tangle of intersecting lines. The web began to shift. The wormhole led to a galaxy, which appeared to be the Milky Way. Spindle was halfway across the room—

"Danger, Will Robinson. Danger."

Spindle stopped. His eyelight circled around to the back of his head. Streeter's projected image was standing next to me.

"Get it?" he asked. "Lost in Space? Will Robinson?" He looked back and forth between Spindle and me. "You mean you guys never heard of that ancient TV show with the robot? They did the remake." He did robot-arms. "*Danger.*"

"Why is Master Streeter projecting into our meeting?" Spindle asked.

"I'm sorry," I said, trying to stop Streeter from doing the robot. "I forgot I scheduled him to come over."

Actually, I forgot completely. A small wave of panic swept through me. Spindle was right, I'm losing focus.

"Did I drop in on something top secret?" he asked.

The wormhole network was public knowledge, but I still thought Spindle might shoot that eye-laser. I calmed Streeter down, asked Spindle to keep going. I should've told Streeter to leave, but he was making me laugh. Maybe I was delirious. It just felt good to smile.

"Do you think this is a joke, Master Socket?"

"No, Spindle."

Streeter waited quietly, like listening to parents fight. I knew this stuff was important, but I needed a break. Streeter was exactly what I needed. Just seeing his image lifted the fatigue. I think Spindle picked up on that. There were still important matters at hand, but he could feel the tension relax inside me.

"Can we cover the destination?" I asked. "I'll work with the ship-integration focus later today."

He agreed. He followed the wormhole to a planet on the outskirts of the Milky Way. It was not a long trip, not by intergalactic standards.

When Spindle touched a planet that swirled red, white and blue, the wormholes vanished, leaving us in the dark for a moment. Then the room projected the planet's atmosphere, like we were standing right there on the surface.

It was a bleak environment. The sky was steely. The distant mountains were red and the surface gritty. The few trees that sprouted here and there on the flat plain were enormous, but they had no leaves. Instead, their bright green bark was photosynthetic.

"Your destination is the Grimmet Outpost." Spindle pointed to the enormous dome-shaped structure that appeared between us and the mountains, the white surface looked pink with red dust. "Your ship will land directly inside the Outpost and you will be greeted by the Paladin crew that resides there. You will not be venturing out of the Outpost since that would require further training and fitted gear. You will be tested for signs of fatigue and given a tour of the facility before returning home."

"I thought you were going away for a month?" Streeter asked.

"Time does not operate that way, Master Streeter. Since Master Socket will be traveling at the speed of light for a short period, time will slow down for him. While his trip may only seem brief, weeks will pass for us."

Spindle charged into the rest of the visit, who I would be meeting, what we would be doing and what I could expect. Now I was getting sleepy.

A distant flutter echoed from one of the leafless trees. Then a cloud of brightly colored grimmets appeared to be heading for us. When they were close enough to hear their wings, my office projected their images around us. They were as playful as the ones in the Preserve. Maybe the trip wouldn't be so bad.

Streeter walked into the mob with his hands up. It was hard not to join them when they were near, even if it was just a projection. Spindle gave up. He left the office without saying another word. I'd apologize later. In the meantime, Streeter and I would have some fun.

An hour.

I'd been asleep for an hour before waking up with a cold shiver running down my back. No memory of a vision or a dream, just the remnants of one. Maybe it knocked me out again, only this time I was already sleeping. I laid there staring at the ceiling but couldn't remember having a vision, but there was no doubt one had happened. *Now I'm not remembering them?* I was buzzing with adrenaline.

I had transformed my office to replicate the tagghet field, again. I hated that I was getting accustomed to the convenience of it – the sounds and smells were dead-on – because I much preferred the real thing, but I let myself be lazy. I told myself there wasn't time to get out there, but that was bullshit. I just wanted to sit. Now.

I had been sitting for almost an hour, sweat running down my face as the room replicated the humidity. Even though I hadn't eaten in almost a day, I felt full. The longer I sat, the fuller I became. Not full, really. *Dense.*

An hour and a half into sitting, the kids quietly walked in with their cushions and sat with me. A certain joy vibrated between us without a word. I couldn't help but smile as they folded their legs and settled their minds. Soon, our breathing was synchronized and we blended with the surrounding sounds and scents.

The silence was shattered by an earthshaking tremor. Despite the unnatural interruption, none of us broke from our sitting. We remained motionless, but I could feel the thoughts of concern rumble through the office. Finally, Spindle stepped inside. He paused at the entrance and folded his hands in front of his belly. He waited until I looked his way.

"Your escort has arrived, Master Socket."

We sat a few moments longer. The kids didn't move until I gave a short bow. I was sluggish to get off the ground, loosening my joints like my blood had turned to syrup. I gave the kids encouragement to keep up the schedule, that Spindle would be taking care of them, and I'd see them soon. The girls gave me hugs. I held my hand out to shake Ben's hand, but he pulled me in for a hug, patting my back.

"Hugging ain't just for chicks," he said.

I had to laugh and hugged the rest of them. I'd gone on trips before. This felt like a long goodbye. Did they sense the heaviness weighing inside me, sharing my agitation while we sat?

"Tagghet when you get back," Aiesha said. "Don't turn rusty on me, old man."

I was five years older than them, and I was the old man. I was certainly walking like one. I informed Spindle to take them to the tagghet field and I'd meet him down at the launch.

I put on my official space travel outfit. It was dark blue and fitted with numerous pockets and built-in communication modules, thermal-conditioning adjustments to keep my body temperature adequate under extreme conditions, armor-imbedded material to resist impact. Even had a back door to drop a load. I doubled-checked the backpack that contained everything needed for surviving extended periods in the middle of nowhere.

When the office was quiet, I called for the walls to dim the tagghet field projection so I could rest in the darkness for a while. There was just enough light to see the desk. I straightened up some papers, activated messages for anyone contacting me while I was gone and checked over my schedule one more time.

It was too dark to see to the other side of the office. Like my future. I was tempted to call Chute and Streeter one last time, but I'd already said my goodbyes. Instead, I called up Chute's room. Her bed appeared. The covers were thrown back and the pillow dented. She was already about her day.

I needed to do the same.

SHOWTIME

Paladins were lined up in the parking garage. Most just nodded as I passed, some shook my hand, patted me on the shoulder. Servys were hovering in lines behind them. All seemed present and accounted for. The floor was vibrating with the hum of something powerful, pulsing through the bottom of my feet; I could feel it in my teeth. I stepped through the wall to the other side where the ship would be waiting in the boulder field.

I stopped immediately. I'd seen images of these deep space cruisers in my studies, knew what they looked like, but in person it was just... daunting. It was black, oval and smooth, like a skipping stone. And it took up the entire field, almost 300 yards across. There were no windows, none visible at least. The air around it trembled like it was fiercely hot, but it seemed to have more to do with the color, a black totally void of light. The ship seemed to be eating the space around it.

The Commander was standing to the side, letting me take it all in. He nodded at me as if to say, *take your time.*

The vibrations I felt inside the parking garage emanated from the ship, quivering through the ground with a low frequency that penetrated solid granite. They intensified for a moment, like it sensed I was staring. Like it was saying, *yeah, this shit's for real, son.*

"I had no idea it would be this…" I trailed off. I didn't know what I meant. I just had no idea. Period. "This is just for me?"

"You'll be travelling alone," the Commander said.

"Seems a bit much. Couldn't you send something a little…" Again, I wasn't sure if smaller was what I was thinking. *Maybe something a little less bad ass?*

"It takes a lot to travel through space," he said.

"That thing will fit through the wormhole?"

He smiled, but instead of answering he adjusted the straps on my backpack. It weighed over seventy pounds, but my body felt so dense that the backpack felt like a box of tissues. The ship contained everything I needed. The pack was just an insurance policy.

"In case you're wondering, I don't personally see every Paladin off on their first trip." The Commander smacked my back like he was sending off a horse. "But your mother insisted."

"I appreciate that, sir."

He grabbed both shoulders. "This is a routine trip, son. No need to be nervous. You've been through things plenty worse than this." He winked.

He sensed my nervousness. Is that what it was, nervousness? I was feeling as rigid as a flagpole and heavy as a tank. I trusted my gut feelings and this one was saying stay right here, this was not the trip I wanted to take. But something also told me this trip was inevitable. It was now or later. But why did something so routine feel so imminent?

The ship's humming intensified again. A doorway was glowing on the black surface. The Commander patted me again, one more wink. "Godspeed, son."

"Thank you, sir."

I started the slow march toward the doorway, the wind whistling in my ears. Each step was heavy, vibrating every time the bottom of my foot touched the ground like it was a vibratory plate, compacting my insides. The air was becoming dense, like the ship was pushing back the closer I got. Each step took more and more effort.

I thought about turning around and asking the Commander what he thought, but it wasn't the ship pushing against me. It was me; like rigor mortis setting in. Maybe it was those vibrations just whacking me out, getting me ready for the super-squeeze of the wormhole. Like Spindle said, we were going to the other side of the galaxy, not Charleston. Was this prepping me for the ride?

I could feel the cold wave emanating from the ship's surface like it was sucking the energy out of the atmosphere. I had to push my last step through the doorway. First, it was bright and so cold it squeezed out my last breath. But then I was through and the ship was gone. Gone, as in gone-gone.

I was standing in the boulder-field. No ship around me. Everything, completely silent.

There was a table in front of me, round and black like the ship. The surface was smooth. The field silent. The trees moved, but the wind didn't gust in my ears. Birds flew over, their beaks jerking open while their heads searched below. But no caw. I scratched my face and heard my fingertips rub against my skin.

The Commander was still where I left him, hands clasped behind his back. I started to walk back but an invisible force pushed back. I must be inside the ship, the walls projecting the view from the outside so they appeared invisible to me. The Commander would still be seeing the black ship. *Spindle must've missed this detail. Or maybe I wasn't listening.*

I expanded my mind, felt the smooth surface of the invisible walls and the circuitry within them. I merged with the ship's intelligence, sensing its directive to serve. It felt cold and alien. And massive. I opened to the ship's database, allowed it to connect with me and read my intentions. The experience of its artificial intelligence stung with a slight metallic ring. Soon, we were intertwined with a single goal in mind. *The Grimmet Outpost.*

The trees shook violently, whipping leaves into the sky, the grass jerking back and forth. The ground slowly dropped away beneath my feet. I lifted magically into the air. Vertigo swirled in my stomach.

Higher and faster I went. And closer to the cliff. I soared over the top to see tree-covered mountains far in the distance and drifted near a great chasm that was filled with the Preserve. Nothing stirred as I cruised over it, the jungle separated from me by its invisible forcefield. In the middle of the trees was a dark green oval dotted with six children and a silver humanoid, looking up. They were waving.

I drifted further until they blended with the scenery. A lightning bolt, absent of thunder, licked the sky. I was moving near the center of an electrical storm that swirled ahead. It began to open, the center black, swallowing the bands of lightning like it was hungry for our world, growing larger and wider. I felt like plankton being inhaled by a whale. I gripped the table, cold and smooth and solid. Maybe that's why it was there, to keep me from falling over.

The black opening suddenly ripped open, exposing a blue throat. I was swallowed with no time to brace for impact. No time to scream. It was like being sucked through a straw. But just as sudden as my body felt steamrolled, there was no sense of motion. There was no sight or smell. For a long moment, I was bodiless. There was no pressure. No pain. There was nothing.

Getting past the first part was nothing short of being blown to bits. After that, it was the greatest peace I'd ever known. No body, no thoughts. No sense of going anywhere. Maybe this was what death felt like.

But I was moving. Towards destiny.

There was no stopping that. We all arrive where we're going. And as my body began to exit the other end of the wormhole, preceded by the siren scream of my nervous system reminding me that it was working again, I had the nagging thought my destiny was near.

Showtime.

II

Serving life is not always beautiful.
Pivot

A perfect trap is one the prey readily accepts,
even when he already knows the outcome.
Pike

Ye shall know the truth, and the truth shall make you free.
John 8:32

OUTPOST

The exit was as quick as the entrance. For a second, I sensed my body had already arrived at the destination before I did. But I was catching up, arriving in time to feel the wormhole shit me out the other end of that intergalactic straw.

My extremities were cold and my fingers tingling. I blinked several times to focus the blurry details of men, more than one, somewhere in front of me. There was a hollow pain burning inside my chest. I wasn't breathing.

I pulled in my first breath like I was drowning, gasping for air. I bent over and, with my hands on my knees, was ready to puke. It passed, but when I stood up my mouth was filling with spit. I blinked away the tears. Now I could see three men. Maybe they were smiling.

I walked toward them, each step tentative. I couldn't feel the ship's walls anymore, but then again I couldn't feel much of anything. Five feet away from them, I passed through the ship's cold doorway and was bombarded with an earthy smell and the sound of the ship's hissing. And that's when my stomach revolted.

I blew chunks all over. It was mostly green liquid, but I was hands on my knees again, wrenching until it was all over my shoes, the floor and whatever else was below.

Someone slapped my shoulder. "That first trip's a bitch, ain't it?" The others chimed in with laughter.

The man in the middle was the commanding officer. His name was Samuel. He handed me a bottle of water to rinse out my mouth.

"Spit it on the floor," he said, when I looked around with a mouthful. Evidently not their first time greeting a first-timer.

I was expecting the inside of the Outpost to look industrial. Where the ship had landed, that was exactly what it was: all gray walls and concrete floor. The translucent ceiling of the dome was far above, letting pale light through.

The other two guys with the commanding officer introduced themselves as Pepper and Fadden. They showed me the rest of the Outpost. It was a small city, complete with streets lined with elms and maples and houses and warehouses. Mosquitoes buzzed and squirrels chirped. They farmed crops, raised animals while they researched the planet outside the dome.

We walked for hours and never reached the perimeter of the dome. We stopped at the central cafeteria, a gathering place for the settlers. They ate. I didn't.

We sat around for a good hour. People dropped into the conversation until there was a couple dozen. They asked the questions, mostly about life back home. Most of the residents were on extended stay in the Outpost, some had been there half their life. Some even born there. While most of them said they didn't miss it, they were still curious. No one forgets home.

My celebrity status among Paladins was missing a planet millions of miles away. Some had heard of me – the Paladin that defeated the duplicates, *The One Who Sees Clearly*, as the grimmets once named me – but it hardly seemed to matter. That was another planet. This was the Outpost.

The sun was a gray disk as seen through the dome when I was escorted outside Samuel's office, a set of steel doors tightly closed. A few minutes later, they slid open. I ascended a short flight of stairs to an enormous room at the edge of the dome. A large desk was alone in the middle of the empty floor, and beyond that was a panoramic view of the vast plain.

Samuel was at the desk, looking busy and more officer-like than he did when he was laughing at my pukefest. Military tension set my body rigid, waiting to approach. This was the president of the Grimmet Outpost.

"Have a look," he finally said. "I'll be done in a moment."

I relaxed and let my gaze wander. My footsteps echoed in the silence, but the outside world was a dry, whirling windstorm. Dust-devils dropped to the ground, picking up debris and sending it airborne before disappearing as quickly as they formed. There were ancient, leafless trees sparely populating the flat, baked ground, like the ones I saw in my office, and red mountains in the distance. I went up to the dome, put my fingers on the surface. It was warm.

There were no signs of life. A beaten planet. Only a clear barrier that separated life on the inside from death on the outside.

"Quite a view, isn't it?" Samuel stepped next to me.

I nodded, but not convincingly. Captivating, yes. But I failed to see the beauty in a lifeless landscape.

"This is where the grimmets live?" I asked. He nodded. "Up in the mountains?"

"Mostly, yes. They occasionally visit the plains and flock to the Outpost out of curiosity, but we don't see them much. Mostly when we venture out."

The planet didn't look diverse, but it was rich in elements valuable to Earth. Why else be here? The Outpost was just one of many settlements on the planet. Mines were set up all over. They weren't here just to live on another planet. There was profit involved.

"This planet wasn't always dead," Samuel said, gazing out. "There is some water and the atmosphere can support life, but when we discovered it there was none to be found. There is evidence that beings once lived here, the remnants of houses and roads, cities and farming. Signs of advanced civilization. One can only imagine what it looked like when it was still vital."

He was looking at a plume of smoke in the distant mountains.

"I'm sure you're well aware of our mining industry, but our primary objective for being here is research. This is an expensive operation and the mining of energy-rich minerals helps fund our exploration. Those trees you see are some of our first successes. Instead of leaves, the bark is photosynthetic, tolerating the harsh conditions. This is one of the first links in planet-building. Our goal is that one day this planet will be habitable, once again. That many generations from now, the human population can call it a home."

"I don't understand. How could the entire planet be void of life if the atmosphere is habitable? I mean, asteroids or pestilence or war couldn't wipe out *all* life."

"We're not sure." He was still curiously eyeing the mountains. The cloud was dispersing, growing larger and nearer. It didn't appear to be smoke. "All our research indicates that life just vanished. As if a heart just stopped beating. What could do something like that is, currently, beyond our understanding. And that's another reason we're here." He flicked a glance toward me before resuming his watch on the cloud. "If it can happen here, can it happen on Earth?"

I wondered if he was holding back information. We knew so much, how could there be so much mystery about a dead planet?

"What made the grimmets immune?" I asked.

"Tenacious beings. Unlike anything in the universe. They're similar to cold-blooded organisms, going extended periods of time without food. They seem to have some ability to photosynthesize as well as utilize minerals and nutrients from soil, rocks and trees. Somehow, they resisted whatever wiped everything else out. Of course, I don't need to tell you about their psychic ability."

All right, so he was aware of my connection with them. Of course he would know I shared a special bond with grimmets back on Earth.

"But even as tough as they are, their populations are dwindling. We tried to incorporate them into our environment," Samuel said, "inside the Outpost, but it just didn't work. They weren't acclimated to the friendly climate and didn't care to be separated from the flock."

He stared to the distant plume, let his thoughts drift for a moment.

"One day," he said, "this planet will be revitalized. The grimmets will reclaim its wonder. And, hopefully, we'll be able to share that with them."

Long ago, I accused the Paladin Nation of kidnapping grimmets, bringing them back to Earth for selfish reasons, convinced they intended to make a weapon of them or simply display them like zoo animals. Even when the grimmets defeated the duplicates, I assumed that to be a fluke. But now it seemed like an act of compassion, an attempt to preserve their kind until their home was saved.

Perhaps my trip was not just for the wormhole, but to see some of the truly humane aspects of the Paladin Nation.

Samuel dismissed me to return to my escorts with a firm handshake and a warm smile. "You're welcome to return any time you wish. Trust me, the wormhole ride gets easier."

I thanked him and left, but not before noticing that he was still watching the growing cloud. I could feel a slight tug in my gut, like something familiar was coming.

My goodbyes were short. Everyone waved in passing, but life resumed in the Outpost. We walked through the large docking doors into the hangar, the gray room that housed the black wormhole ship where it was cold and sterile.

"In case you're wondering, the trip back is even worse," Pepper said, patting my shoulder. Fadden laughed, mentioned the room still smelled like puke.

I knew what he meant. Now that I knew what to expect, my thoughts were making the anticipation of the trip worse. Even so, there was a pleasant sensation tugging inside my belly and it was getting stronger. I was sure someone would be waiting for me at the ship. Someone I knew.

My backpack was sitting on the floor in front of the doorway glowing on the ship. It was a little fuller than when I arrived, filled with items from the Outpost to take back.

"Come back if you're bored." Pepper extended his hand as the sky seemed to dim. "You don't get a waiting party on your next visit so you'll have to clean up your own barf."

"Thanks," I said, shaking his hand. "You're an excellent host," I said, sarcastically.

"What can I say? By the way, you know when you get back everyone will be about two weeks older. Time's going a little faster for them."

I sensed a bit of sadness. Did he leave anyone behind? No one was immune to homesickness.

"Well, I better get back before they forget me," I said.

Fadden slapped Pepper with the back of his hand. He was looking up, mouth open. The top of the dome was a couple hundred yards above us. Dark lumps could be seen squirming on the opaque surface.

Fadden and Pepper shaded their eyes like that could somehow clarify what they were seeing, but it was just getting darker as more things dropped out of the sky, scratching and clawing along the surface. The dome was too thick and far away to hear anything, but the commotion was frenzied.

"Yeah?" Pepper touched his ear, listening to a nojakk call. "Seriously? No, no. We see it over here, too."

"Check this out." Fadden was squatting on his haunches in front of a thin silver sheet spread out on the floor projecting a three-dimensional image.

It was an aerial image of the Outpost from far up. Thousands of brightly colored things were crawling over it. *Grimmets.* And more were coming. Floating lights kicked on. I looked up at the thick layer of grimmets obscuring every bit of sunlight.

Pepper and Fadden looked at me. They'd never seen anything like it. No one had. Every grimmet within range of the Outpost was coming. *They can feel me.* And I could feel them tugging at my insides, connecting with their energy, their unlimited essence, bonding to me like the grimmets back on Earth.

Strangely, though, I felt they were connecting with something else, like I carried something inside me, something dense. Maybe they came because of that.

What's inside me?

The ship welcomed me with its impatient hum. I could see through its invisible walls, once again. Pepper and Fadden waited far away from the ship. They didn't bother waving. Didn't seem concerned about the white-blue light that crackled behind me, illuminating their faces. They'd seen the wormhole open inside the Outpost too many times to be amazed. I stayed still, not wanting to see it swallow me. Braced for impact.

My teeth snapped together, just missed clipping my tongue. I was pulled into oblivion, once again, with my mind focused on home, guiding the ship back to the warm life that waited with familiar surroundings and loving friends and family.

The black nothingness of the moment was peaceful. It didn't feel like I was moving, but I sensed home was near. My destination began to pull me back into existence, like my body had been evaporated and was being reconstructed inside Earth's atmosphere somewhere over the Preserve. I sensed oncoming pain.

I was jerked in another direction like a fish snagged with a treble hook.

I went back into the black peaceful oblivion, but home felt like it was far behind. But then I felt my body again, reassembling somewhere near the planet. And then there was the excruciating agony as my awareness squeezing back into it.

My eyes were clenched as tightly as my jaw. I was mostly numb, again, but felt water slosh around me.

I moved my arms in a swimming motion, unaware if I was below water or not. My lungs burned. I opened my eyes, the salty water stinging. Panic propelled me upward but I was too heavy. My arms were like useless poles. I desperately kicked and barely broke the surface, inhaling just enough air to relieve the fire in my chest. But I sank again.

There was no chance of getting back up, but fortunately I hit the sandy bottom. I pushed upward, this time clearing my entire chest above the water. One deep gulp of air and I let myself sink again. I pushed off at an angle but found the water getting deeper, so I turned around, jumping again and again.

Finally, I stood on my toes and gulped air. My heart was slamming. I took feeble steps and slowly walked into shallower water.

A sandy beach was ahead. The full moon was bright in a clear night sky. I missed my landing. But I had no idea by how much.

SILENT FOREST

Something flushed out of my body, like a plug had been pulled and drained molten metal weighing in my veins. I was light as driftwood. The water around me turned cloudy. I rubbed my eyes and looked again. The milky cloud drifted deeper and spread out like an oil slick.

When I reached dry sand, I dropped to my knees. Exhausted. I was catching my breath, the air cool and humid. Seawater dripped off my nose, over my lips. It tasted odd. It was salty, but there was something else, something familiar. Something that usually wasn't associated with ocean water, but I couldn't place it.

There was no sign of civilization. Just endless water, sand and tropical trees. This was bad. It could've been worse. The north pole. Or the sun.

I tapped my cheek, got no response from my nojakk. Not even a tick, tick, tick. I dug through my backpack, activated a handheld phone but it was non-responsive, too. The same with a homing beacon. Everything, dead.

Maybe an electromagnetic pulse killed everything upon entry. Something went wrong right before I got home, I felt it jerk me around. Maybe the ship malfunctioned and dumped me in the ocean. At least it didn't drop another twenty feet out to sea or I'd be stuck to the bottom like an anchor.

My suit had already dried. I sat down in the sand, leaned back against a tree. *What now? Surely, the Paladins knew I was coming back. They would eventually search for me. But if I didn't have power to signal them, how would they find me?*

The waves were small, sloshing onto the beach in a steady rhythm. I closed my eyes, listening to the ocean go in and out. In and out.

It lulled me to relax, but something was missing. Everything felt so... so empty. Like an environment in my office where nothing was real. But I couldn't sense any walls. I considered, for a second, that I was in my office. But I could always sense the confines of a moldable environment, sense the walls of a room even though it looked endless. The beach had no such limitation. It just felt empty.

Maybe I imagined it. I was tired.

The waves greeted me gently. I imagined I was floating in the water, warm and cozy. But then I opened my eyes and stared at coconuts. My survival suit was warm but the cool air was nipping at my ears and the tip of my nose. I sat up and rubbed my face. My eyes were heavy with sleep. I couldn't remember laying down. The moon hung just above the horizon. It felt like I'd been asleep for hours, but everything looked the same. And not a single bug bite.

It was quiet in the trees. Too quiet. The only thing that broke the silence was the ocean, but everything else was as still as a museum. No breeze from above, no drifting leaves or scuttle of a crab. Absolute stillness.

The backpack contained small packets of food. If that ran out, there was a supply of lifepatches that could sustain me for another six months. If I hunt and gather, I could survive for much longer.

The forest looked dense and dark. It would take a long, sharp machete to cut through it. Since there was no such thing in the backpack, I walked along the beach looking for a path. But after a few miles, everything still looked exactly the same. In fact, even the trees appeared in some sort of pattern. Up ahead was a palm that leaned and curved skyward. I turned back, swore I passed one like that a few miles back.

Just beyond that was a small opening that gave way to a narrow path. That wasn't there before. I looked out over the water one last time. The night sky looked black and smudged just above the horizon, like ink was leeching up from the water.

I had pulled small box from the backpack and let it unfold into a tent. I lay inside it, staring through the dome-shaped ceiling. I couldn't see the sky through the trees. The moonlight filtered through the leaves like pale sunlight. I had walked for what seemed a full day and expected the sun to come up, but I was exhausted and couldn't wait for it any longer.

The forest was endless and repetitive. The path continued to wind through it like something or someone walked it often enough to beat down the vegetation, but there was no sign of life. Nothing. No spider webs or mosquitoes or stinging ants.

It was still cool, but humid as ever. I sweated through much of my water reserves and there wasn't much left in the backpack. I needed to find some before long.

I woke when a single drop of water struck the tent.

The raindrop jiggled, then slowly made its way down the side, racing to the bottom. Something about that was strange, then I realized that was the first sound in a day that I hadn't directly caused.

It was darker outside. Maybe clouds had dimmed the moonlight. *Wait. Did I sleep through another day?*

I felt rested, like I'd gotten another eight hours of sleep but it was still night. Was I sleeping right through the daylight?

Maybe it was for the best. I didn't need to be moving around in the heat of the day. I was already parched.

Another day of hiking. Still no sunlight.

I don't know how far I got. Thirty miles, maybe. The last ten miles were like wearing concrete blocks. Raindrops continued to find a way through the thick canopy. My lips were cracking and I'd stopped sweating. I finished the rest of my water.

I sat against a tree.

Thunder clapped.

I woke in a thick mass of groundcover. No tent. I must've fallen over asleep.

Rain dripped through a fern leaf, splashing on my forehead. I stuck out my tongue, caught the next drop. And the next.

They were plopping throughout the forest with a regular beat. I scrambled on my hands and knees and found a large leaf holding a pool of water. Carefully, I cupped it and tilted it toward my mouth. It was wet, tasteless. Just like water was suppose to taste. If this was some sort of moldable environment, I wouldn't be able to drink it.

The lifepatches kept me from dehydrating, but water was a better alternative, so I spent the next couple hours going leaf to leaf, scavenging what I could.

The path continued to curve through the otherwise impenetrable forest. It seemed endless and pointless, but it had to lead somewhere. Something made this path. Maybe I should've stayed on the beach. At least a search party would see me there. Nothing would spot me through the trees. Too late now. I just had to keep going until I got out or found someone that could help.

I only managed an hour on the trail before I had to rest. I was drained. And sleepy. These were tough conditions, but this was unusual. I shouldn't be gassing out this quick. It was like something was sucking the energy out of me; reminded me of the Grimmet Outpost. *Like something just sucked the life out of it.*

I slapped another lifepatch on my neck, felt it pump essential nutrients into my jugular. Thunder rumbled somewhere in the distance. I remembered something my grandma used to tell me about storms. She said when it thundered, the angels were wrestling.

The ground began to tremor like they'd fallen out of the sky.

Maybe it was the third night that I saw the end.

The winding path straightened out and widened. There was an opening in the trees. I quickened my pace, eager to find something. The trees ended abruptly, like a wall, and the path dropped down a steep slope. I stood just inside the canopy, mesmerized by the view. Hills rolled off into the distance covered in tufts of grass. Mountains were farther out.

The air was cooler and drier. The moon was still full, but the sky seemed hazy. On the horizon, the ink stain was still visible. It was deep and dark, blotting out the stars as it bled further into the night sky.

Below me, a couple hundred yards out, the grass gave way to rows of fruit trees. Something moved among them. It was a woman. Her clothes were white, her hair blonde. She was picking fruit and putting them into a basket.

Finally, a way home. I screamed through my hands but she didn't hear me. I didn't bother shouting again, instead I started down the path. Adrenaline filled me with excitement and burst with renewed energy. I'd catch up to her in minutes. Maybe I could find home by sunrise. The thought of sleeping in my office boosted my stride down the slope. I ignored the thought lurking in my head, the nagging concern that had been with me ever since I walked out of the water. Something I tried to reason away because help was finally within reach.

Why does everything still feel so empty?

EMPTY ANGEL

Still raining, maybe a bit harder.

I wasn't about to let the woman out of my sight. I left the winding path and took the grassy hill full speed, leaping over boulders. I lost sight of her as I dipped into the valley, cresting the hill to once again see the magnificent view.

The forest behind me seemed further away than it should've been. I'd only been running a few minutes and it was hundreds of yards back.

A subtle breeze, the first I could remember since arriving, caught my attention. It carried the fragrance of tea olive blossoms and the salty spray of an ocean. And the scent of a woman, soft and loving. She was there, I could see her on the next hill in the orchard, still hundreds of yards away. I hadn't gotten any closer.

Her white gown fluttered while she stopped to reach into a tree, pulling fruit from a branch and putting it in her basket. She was glowing, like a beam of moonlight found its way through the rain to touch only her. I cupped my hands and shouted again. "HELLO!"

Still couldn't hear me.

I started down the next grassy hill into the orchard. The trees were taller than I thought. My perspective seemed off. The trunks were gnarly and the muscled branches held plump apples the size of softballs. I lost sight of the woman as she walked over the next hill. But I was gaining on her. I dipped my head, pushed harder. I reached the next hilltop, expecting to maybe catch her while she went searching in another tree, maybe only a few yards away. At the very least she'd be within shouting distance, but then saw her still hundreds of yards out.

I stopped, put my hands on my knees. How did she get that far out?

My heart pounded. The adrenaline was already wearing off and I was sweating out precious water that mixed with the rain dripping down my face, leaving a salty tang on my lips.

This isn't logical. Where am I?

When I looked up, as if answering my questions, the view had somehow changed. Had I not noticed it when I emerged from the forest? Was it just hidden from my vantage point? Because now, beyond the rolling hills, was a vast black ocean. The lines of orchard trees followed the undulating hills, ending short of a massive house built right on the shore, surrounded by sand dunes and sea oats.

The woman was gone.

The sterile forest and the perfect temperature, short of the rain this is paradise. This exists nowhere in nature. Nowhere on Earth. I looked at my hands, turned them over and studied them like the truth was written somewhere on my skin. I'm not dreaming or virtualmode. I'm here, in the skin.

I turned back and saw what I expected. The trees were gone. Nothing but rising and falling mounds as far as I could see. This entire environment was transforming, manipulating me toward the house on the beach. Something changed when it started to rain, like it let me out of the forest. Once again, I opened my mind to connect with the environment, searching for something substantial, something real, but everything felt empty. So beautiful, but so empty.

The house already seemed bigger. More inviting.

Why does it feel like no matter what direction I walk, I'll end up at the house?

The wicker basket was nestled in the grass at the base of a tree. I picked one of the fruits out. It was deep red, almost purple. The skin was soft but not fuzzy. I press my thumb into it, juice squirting out. Saliva filled into my mouth. It was clear liquid, not milky.

I tossed it on the ground. First, I needed to find the woman. She was in the house.

The house grew as I approached, building onto itself, forming walls and floors and windows until it was a monstrosity blocking out the ocean. Wide steps led to thick double doors, both open and waiting. Sand ground beneath my boots as I crossed over the marble threshold and passed through the doors.

It was one enormous room filled with credenzas, sofas and antique furniture. The walls were covered with art from various eras, from Victorian to modern, realistic to abstract. Expensive vases, candelabras, and sculptures were set about. All in all, a stunning display, but nothing compared to the back wall made entirely of glass, offering a full view of the scenic ocean and the darkening sky. A single fruit tree grew behind the house, its limbs heavy with fruit.

Multi-folding doors were pushed all the way open, leaving wide open access to the beach. I stopped, just short of the beach that extended right up to the house. The breeze came off the water moist and ragged, blowing my hair off my shoulders. *I've seen this place.*

Sand. Rain.

A blackened sky.

The realization rang inside me like I'd been struck by a two-handed mallet. It's where I saw Chute attack, slashing down with a knife. *The vision is taking shape.*

I went outside. The rain was colder, pelting my cheeks. I tensed, looking in both directions for Chute and her knife, but it was empty. I walked further out until the foamy water wrapped around my ankles. And then I saw the woman, far down on my left.

She was standing with her feet in the water, a faint figure blurred by the rain. Her arms were crossed and she was staring out to sea like she was waiting. I could feel her yearning. It was the first thing I'd felt since arriving. Just to experience something real, a quiver of reality, jolted me with excitement.

I started after her but, with each step, she got no closer. The ground moved under my feet, but the back of the house was still exactly where I exited, like the beach was a treadmill.

Thunder clapped without any sign of lightning. The woman was still there, yearning for what was out on the empty water where waves were beginning to swell. Or maybe her gaze was settled on the ink-stained sky.

I walked in the other direction and watched the house. Same thing: it didn't move even though my tracks continued far behind me.

Enough. I'm not entertainment.

Understand your environment, one of the first lessons I learned as a Paladin. Without understanding your Self or your surroundings, you are a ship sailing without a compass.

I tracked puddles into the house. The pillows on the nearest couch were soft velvet, but firm. I centered the largest one near the opening on the back wall and folded my legs.

My breathing quickly became rhythmic while I settled into the present moment. Soon, thoughts faded away. I was aware of the objects around me, the emptiness of the house and angry sea. Occasionally, the sky cracked with thunder.

I would sit in the moment until something, or someone, revealed the truth.

Where am I?

Hours went by.

There was nothing but the steady rhythm of the rain, the rise and fall of my chest and the occasional bump of the tree banging its fruit-laden branch against the glass wall. The waves had taken on a foamy white crest. I had no expectations, made no effort to escape where I was. I just remained open.

And the world remained empty and mysterious.

I sensed a faint presence of another being somewhere in this world, likely the woman, but I couldn't feel exactly where she was. It was like she was everywhere. And out there, somewhere, was somebody besides the woman. It was a man, his presence somewhere on the horizon.

My back ached and my legs became numb. Thirst burned my throat. I considered finding water, but there would be none. The fruit hung tantalizingly.

I sat. The rain continued.

And the fruit continued to knock on the glass like a stranger, wanting to come inside. The metaphor was all too obvious.

Paradise.

The Tree of Knowledge.

Thump. Thump-thump. The fruit said yes.

The splinter of glass woke me.

I'd fallen off the cushion. My tongue was like a piece of meat stuck in my mouth. I tried to swallow. I couldn't remember passing out.

I glimpsed the woman standing in front of me, holding out the fruit. I blinked and she wasn't there. I was hallucinating, but now my mouth was full of saliva. I could smell the fruit, its tangy citrus scent penetrating the humid breeze blowing off the storm-ridden coast.

My head was on the floor, pain pulsing through my ear. I scratched at the floorboards. Waves were punishing the beach, pushing closer to the house. The window was cracked where the tree branches smacked the house, swinging the heavy fruit like a wrecking ball.

She wants me to eat the fruit. I'll die right here on the floor like a dog, shrivel up like a salted slug, before I eat it.

But I didn't die.

I kept on living.

The agony wiped out any thoughts of home. Of Chute, the kids, my mother. I was just writhing on the floor, doubled over as dehydration cramps pull me into a fetal position. Sometimes I heard the rain and thunder and the constant banging. I could feel the hardness of the floor.

I could also hear voices. The woman was calling. I sensed the man out there, too. He was just watching.

And I imagined the taste of the fruit.

This seemed to go on forever.

And then it was there, on the floor in front of me. The fruit was as red as a shined apple. I was dreaming of reaching for it. I didn't have that kind of strength, the kind to even slide my hand across the floor, but then I felt it in my palm and sensed the promise of life inside it. I punctured the skin with my fingertips, watched the sweet juice dribble onto the floorboards. My throat contracted.

I touched my tongue to the fleshy skin of the fruit, the sweetness ignited the taste buds in my mouth. Inside me, rapture exploded.

I devoured it like a starving beast, juice flowing down my chin, the meaty pulp sliding down my throat, filling me, scintillating my nerves. I sucked at my fingers and licked the drippings off the floor. I could smell the ocean wafting into the house along with a loving presence. I heard soft laughter.

It was no dream.

She tricked me. I couldn't resist it any longer. In the end, I willfully took it. But now I was thinking clearly. I knew where I was because eating the fruit had connected me with this world. It was no longer empty. It was real. It made sense.

This isn't Earth.

A HAPPY FAMILY

The truth.

I was pulled from the wormhole just before arriving home, redirected to another part of the universe and absorbed into an alien world. I didn't know how or why it happened, but I knew this much: *this world is artificial.*

The entire planet was composed of cellular nanomechs that formed everything I saw and touched, heard and tasted. That wasn't the sky above. Not sand or water or rain. Not even a tree. It was just the generic stuff made to look like those things. It was my office on a global scale. How this was even possible I did not understand. All I knew was that I was somewhere inside it.

I knew these things because I had eaten the fruit, partaken of this world, and now I was merging with it. That's how I knew these things. My being –my essence, *my soul* – was interweaving with this artificial world. I was becoming one with it.

This was no ordinary automated world, either. It was not like my office that only responded to my commands. There was an intelligence that was inseparable from it, a feminine being fused into every single nanomech, as if she was this world. It was her will that formed the ocean, and grew the trees, her will that sent the moon across the sky. She was everywhere.

That feminine energy was in the room. The woman in white was standing just inside the house, facing the torrential storm. Her arms were crossed, her fingers drumming her biceps.

"Manumit is making quite a mess," she said, without turning.

Manumit. I knew who she was talking about. There was another presence in this world that was separate from her. He was the reason the sky was black. Why it was raining in paradise. She called him Manumit, but now I recognized this presence. I'd known him all my life. *Pivot*.

"Who are you?" I asked.

"You know who I am."

I knew this world, how it worked, that it was artificial. But I didn't know her. Didn't know her thoughts, where she came from. Why she was part of it.

"You don't know everything?" She smirked.

She knew my thoughts, taunting me with her secret. I didn't even know her name.

"Fetter," she said. "Manumit called me Fetter. And he calls you Socket. You call him Pivot." She looked at me over her shoulder. Her eyes were blue like the deep part of the ocean. "Aren't we one big happy family?"

I pushed off the floor. There were no aches or numbness. I felt in total control of my nervous system. In fact, I felt like I could move the environment with a thought like fingers and toes. I looked at a footstool and willed it to slide near me. It came to a stop in front of me. I contracted my awareness, trying to disconnect from the environment.

I'm becoming this world. Like her.

"I'm not staying here." I said it like that would make it true, like I would wake up if I heard myself say it.

She smirked, again. "Have a seat, make yourself comfortable and I'll tell you everything you don't know." She strolled over to the right where there was now an open kitchen. She pulled the silver door of the refrigerator and said while she searched inside, "And some things you don't want to know."

"I'm fine standing."

"You sure?"

Lightning struck nearby. Glasses clinked on the counter and the woman named Fetter pulled liquor bottles from below the counter, began mixing drinks. She looked up because I was staring. Smiled.

"You know, if you just open to me I won't have to explain it. You'll know the truth for yourself. You know as well as I do, darling, the truth is always waiting for us. We just have to open to it."

I felt the texture of the transforming world and Pivot crashing through it, but I was holding back, even if I couldn't disconnect. She cocked her head like she was thinking *have it your way* and took a sip.

She poured a bit more liquor in one glass then prepared a plate of cheese and crackers, carried them over to the long leather couch facing the ocean. She placed coasters on the antique table and put the drinks down. She patted the seat next to her.

"That's for you." She slid the drink a few inches in my direction.

"No."

"Suit yourself."

She sipped the drink that simulated a euphoric sensation. Even though she could make herself feel that way by willing it, she preferred the process of drinking. Maybe she wanted to feel human. Or maybe she was nervous and needed to rely on old habits. Her energy quivered with a subtle hint of doubt while she watched the storm. It wasn't the weather she contemplated, it was Pivot. He was doing this.

"We made this world, darling." She pondered a bit more. "We have existed, Manumit and I, for an eternity. I know that doesn't make sense to your mind, how can we exist forever? But you'll understand that time is relative when you truly blend with the universe. This planet was our home. And now that he's back, it's our home once again."

She nibbled on a cracker. I was motionless.

"I know this doesn't make sense. Trust me, you'll understand with time. Right now, just accept what I'm saying and stay open to the truth. The details of how we did this are irrelevant. What's important is how the story began."

She pointed her drink at the weather before taking a sip.

"It's a love story, darling. True love. Manumit is my yang. I'm his ying. Together, we're one. Apart," she gestured again to the storm, "we're chaos."

She savored the taste on her tongue and gazed outside, lovingly. Then I understood. *She's the ying. The night.* I hadn't been sleeping through the day. It was continually night in this world. Pivot was the day. Had it been night since he left?

"Night and day," she said. "Yes, you're beginning to understand."

"Good and evil?"

"Perhaps. Although good and evil are human concepts. Evil often results from a lack of understanding, and humans lack plenty of that. Your mind is still too human to comprehend what I mean. Dark and light, that makes more sense."

Lightning illuminated her face. She had everything she could possibly want. Even now, she was enjoying the brewing storm, even though she couldn't control it. But if all this were true, if she was exactly what I thought she was, if she was this entire world and if indeed I wasn't dreaming, then what else was there to desire? Maybe the unpredictability of the weather was something new. Finally, something she could experience that was outside herself. How lonely it must've been when everything she experienced was herself. No one to share it with. She needed Pivot.

But still, this was all artificial. And so was she. She was like the intelligence that molded the walls of my office, only she was self-aware. She could choose how to mold it. And now she was

104

saying Pivot was artificial, too. That, somehow, he always has been.

"You're not real," I said. "This is all an illusion; it may as well be a dream. You're making your own reality. Your delusions feed themselves. You're a machine that believes it's real."

The furniture chattered like an earthquake rumbled underground. Fetter's face darkened for a moment. Maybe, for just a second, she saw the truth, that I was right, that she was a just a dream. That if she woke up to the realization of her true nature she would disappear and the only way she could exist was to stay asleep and keep dreaming.

"We're more than real, darling." She said it like she was including me. The rosy glow returned to her cheeks. "You don't know just how real. Not yet."

She walked towards me and gently ran the back of her fingers down my cheek, smiling. Her fragrance was intoxicating, like a morning after a thunderstorm of vanilla-scented blossoms.

She walked around the room, paused at an abstract painting that hung over a monstrous fireplace. The oily colors were a montage of seemingly random swipes that swirled with emotion.

"We were once human, in a sense. Long ago," she said. "But we became gods."

"You're artificially infused into this world. You're nothing more than technology. You're more like a program and you know this. You didn't create that painting, you only copied it from a memory. It's a duplication of a Pollack."

She stood in front of the painting a bit longer before walking to the center of the room to sit at a grand piano that wasn't there a minute ago. She softly played.

"It's like a duplicated human, I suppose?" It was a question, but she posed it like a statement. *Think about that.*

She knew that humans had managed to convert their bodies to inorganic machines composed of nanotechnology, cell-sized machines that imitated organic bodies. Their memories, their consciousness, were implanted into these bodies and they existed like they were alive. They thought and breathed and bled like they were still human. But they wouldn't get sick, would not succumb to disease or the whims of the environment because they could will their bodies to do what they wanted. Fetter was saying that, yes. She was like a duplicated human, only her body was a planet!

But duplications lacked a soul. They weren't real. And they knew, somewhere deep inside, that they were artificial and lacked what their human lives contained: *beingness*. Inside, they were hollow. They craved realness.

Was that what Fetter was claiming? Did the fact that her body was an entire planet made her feel less hollow? Did it make her feel more real?

"Believing you're a god does not make you one."

"Gods build planets." She pounded out an intimidating series of keys. *Dum, dum, dum, DUH.* "We create whatever we desire. We create ourselves. I believe that is the definition of a god. Look it up."

A dictionary appeared on the coffee table to my left.

"Is that any different than dreaming?" I asked.

"Perhaps dreams are the reality." She raised her eyebrows then immersed herself in a classical piece that seemed to dance with the storm. She suddenly stopped, looked at me. "Have you ever loved?"

I didn't answer. Her questions were patronizing. She already knew my thoughts. I attempted to close my mind, hide from her prying mind but I was too tightly integrated with the world. *With her.*

"Of course, you have." Her fingers played softly, again. "It's okay to love, it's not a weakness. It requires courage to be open to whatever the other person brings. When you love, *truly* love, you are willing to risk everything. Pleasure. Pain."

Her fingers ran up and down the keyboard. "Manumit left me." She played the same pattern of notes in a low octave. "He hurt me. I have been unbalanced ever since. I have been alone."

"Why not just create him? If you're God."

She smiled. "Because he came back, darling."

106

Thunder clapped. "He wants to destroy you."

"He can no more destroy me than the universe can end. I can exist in a speck of dust, or the center of a star. I can be reduced to a single byte of information and survive, darling. And from that tiny byte," she stopped playing and held her finger and thumb an inch apart, "I can become whole again. Manumit knows this, he's just acting out because he knows I won't let him leave again."

"Then why am I here? You've got what you want, let me go home. If you know what it's like to lose love, why make me suffer the same?"

She smiled, again. She was hiding something, but instead of telling me her secret she lost herself in Beethoven's *Fifth Symphony*. She hammered the keys and, finally, ended with a furious run that coincided with a bolt of lightning that crawled across the horizon.

"I want to go home."

"You are home, darling."

Nightmare. This has to be Pike. I'm not here. This feels like reality, but this is too insane. I've been in alternate reality before with my real body back on Earth. Is that what's happened? I'm lying on the floor of my office in some sort of catatonic state, foaming at the mouth while Paladin minders try to revive me. Pike gets the last laugh.

"I assure you, Pike has not created this reality," she said.

"Wouldn't my hallucination say that?"

She shrugged. "Do you believe you are dreaming?"

"I've been fooled before."

She looked at me while her fingers danced over the keys and then finally stopped. She stood. "Let's go for a walk."

"I'm not going anywhere."

She neared me and, once again, her presence, her fragrance swayed me like a siren's song. "You've always been a truth-seeker, darling, even when the truth is inconvenient. I know that about you. I know *everything* about you. So I think it's time you know something about yourself that you don't know. What'd you say?" She hooked her arm in mine. "It's a nice night for a walk."

The sky looked like boiling tar and rain fell like bullets. She guided me outside, onto the beach. The raindrops drove into my scalp. I was soaked in seconds. The waves were crashing loudly, non-stop, one after another. Fetter, though, tipped her head back and laughed.

We strolled down the beach, but this time the house receded. I saw the rolling hills off to my left each time a bolt of lightning snapped across the sky. The waves were violent, but nothing like the one welling inside me. Something big was coming. This is just a dream, I tell myself.

"You see, I sensed Manumit near me when you were travelling through that wormhole." She spoke loud enough to be heard over the rain that pounded the hardpacked surf like it was storming gravel. "It had been so long since I felt him. I thought he was coming home, or maybe he was just thinking about it and was near enough for me to hear him. So I took hold of him. I have that ability, darling, to stretch my will across the universe. I brought him home before he changed his mind. I brought him here, back home. But then I realized it was you that I had grabbed. Imagine my surprise."

She squeezed my arm tighter and leaned against me, something Chute had done a hundred times when we walked side by side. Fetter knew this, wanted me to feel more comfortable. More open.

"But I wasn't wrong," she said. "I had gotten Manumit, after all. It turned that you were carrying him inside you and that's why I sensed him. And when you arrived, you released him into the ocean."

Yes. The dense feeling. The release in the ocean and the cloud spreading in the water. And the slow stain on the sky that had become this monsoon. That was Pivot. Somehow, he was inside me. *But how could I carry him?*

"I'll admit, I was confused, at first. Why would my soul-mate use you to deliver him when he has always been welcome to return on his own? But then he refused to integrate with me, insisted on remaining separate from me, from our home. He's caused all this chaos." She held out her hand like she was trying to feel the rain that was dripping off every part of our bodies. "So I left you to wander in the wilderness until I understood his exact intentions."

We walked a bit more. The cold was sinking inside me and I shivered. Fetter's touch was warm.

"And then it all became clear. I understood why my love had gone away. You see, he never left me, darling. He simply went out to find me a gift." She stopped, took my hands. Behind her, the sky was as black as the water, illuminated only by the lightning. Her eyes seemed to glitter. "He brought you."

My breathing stalled. She didn't need to say it. She let her thoughts out in the open and I saw the truth. I knew the secret she had been hiding.

"Our son."

THE LIE AND THE LIAR

Sometimes, you just know things.

You can't explain how. You just see them and know they are truth. *You know it.* When she took my hands, she opened my awareness. Once I believed I was *The One that Sees Clearly.* But it became apparent I was blind.

Now I see.

Our son. Because I'm like them. I am artificial. I'm not fucking real.

Just like them.

It made sense, now. It was how I easily merged into this planet. How I was able to carry Pivot inside me like data. It was how I had been so exceptional among humans. I was the one that extinguished the duplicate race. I was the only one that could see them because I'm one of them. But I couldn't see myself. I was so perfectly human – with my flaws, my ability to love – that no one suspected I was duplicated. That I wasn't human. Not even me.

I couldn't see where I was going. Water was around my ankles. The next wave crashed into my knees. I fell. But I got back up again. The house was a smattering of lights. I wasn't going inside, I'd run past it, maybe into the mountains. There was no escape. But I'd still keep running.

Another wave. This one hit me waist high and began dragging me out. The undertow pulled me down and I let it. But a strong pair of hands latched around my wrists before the sea could fill my lungs.

Fetter lifted me like a child.

I coughed up salty water, my legs weak and wobbly. She led me towards the house. I tried to yank away.

"No. I'm not. I'm not you... I'm just, I'm caught in this... THIS SELF-CENTERED DREAM!"

I twisted my arms, sidestepping and wrenching out of her grip. My back was to the house. The lights lit her face. She looked sad, almost tired. Almost compassionate.

"I know this is hard," she said, much like my mother once said to me. "Your whole life has been a lie. You've been told you're something else and that's not easy to accept. But you'll understand, darling. With time. Just stay open, you'll understand."

It took all my strength to resist her, to stop from going to her, to feel her embrace. Not as a lover, but as a mother. She wanted me to accept the truth. She didn't want to see me in pain, didn't want me to suffer. She wanted me to accept her. To accept this planet. This reality. *Her* reality.

Why would Pivot do this? Why would he keep this secret? Why isn't he here, right now, standing next to her? If I don't open and accept this reality, will this world stay out of balance? Will it be chaos until I do?

"Let day follow the night," she whispered.

"This isn't real."

"Only if you don't accept it."

"Acceptance doesn't make it real."

112

I wiped the rain from my face. There was nowhere to go. *But I'll never accept this place, I'll never open to a world that—*

"Socket?"

Chute.

"Listen, I know this is hard to understand, but you're exactly where you need to be. I'm here. We can be together, here forever. And ever. You know it's all I've ever wanted."

Suddenly, my chest became hot, warming my belly. She pushed her wet hair from her face, her slim fingers freckled like her cheeks. I sensed the familiar essence of Chute, like it was her. *It's really her.* I want to take her, feel her warmth against me—

"No." I shivered.

"It's me, Socket." She reached out, took my hand. Her essence jolted inside me, shook a sob from my throat. I wanted to go to her. "It's me."

My vision. Is that what it is? We're here, in this planet, visiting some stump with a flower?

I won't accept this. I won't.

I tightened my mind, shrank from the goodness, the warmth of the women standing with me in the rain. None of this was true. I'm not artificial. This world is not possible. I would wake up. I'd survive this hallucination and wake up—

"YOU FUCKING LIAR!" Chute slammed the edge of her hand into my windpipe. "You're going to leave me out here, alone? So that you can keep pretending that none of this is real? You going to fucking lie to yourself forever while I sit out here alone, is that what love is to you? Is that how you're going to treat me?"

My throat swelled, my breath wheezing through it. Chute's face was red, her hands clenched at her sides.

"Do you feel the pain?" Fetter asked. "Is that not real? Did you not feel pleasure, love's warmth when you saw her?"

Chute's face softened. Her hands relaxed. Suddenly, I felt the urge to take her, again. But then I stood taller, swallowed. I shook my head, unable to speak. A sense of peace filled me.

Lightning glinted off the silver blade slicing through the air. Chute brought it down. *The vision is fulfilled.* I only had time to raise my hand. The blade cut through my outstretched fingers, cleanly severing them at the knuckles. There was a dull pinch, followed by sudden numbness. The fingers of my right hand tumbled into the water that receded around our ankles.

At first, there was only the white meat of muscle and the gleam of bone. Then the blood came, warmly. The rain washed it away, but didn't stem the flow that poured into my palm.

I circled around, walked backwards towards the sea while shock weakened my knees.

Fetter grabbed my wrist before I could cradle my hand. "Focus, darling. You can be new again."

I stepped back, further into the encroaching water.

"Open to your true nature," she said. "You are not human. You can be whatever you want."

Her grip was too strong. I simply fell to my knees, sinking into the shifting sand.

"Accept your true nature, darling."

I tried to resist her words, but the pain striped away my resistance. I felt the angry nerves at the end of my bloody stumps. I felt the torn flesh and muscle. I'm present with it, connected with it. Not separate.

"There you go," she said, softly. "Whatever you want."

I willed the flesh to rebuild, the muscles to regenerate. The nerves to branch out. I wanted it to stop; I didn't want it to be true. But I couldn't deny true nature.

And just as I willed the flesh and nerves to become new, the blood stopped. Lightning flashed and the stumps elongated. I felt the sting of fresh nerves and new flesh. Knobby knuckles formed and fingernails grew. The skin was lighter than before. It was new.

"Ask," she said, "and you shall receive in this world."

Humans can't regenerate. I can.

"Welcome home. Son."

Truth.

It's not open to interpretation. It just is.

If this is a hallucination, then I accept it as reality. I feel it. I am it. It is my new reality.

The last shreds of resistance gave way. I opened to Fetter, felt her presence swarm inside me. No more separation. *I am this world.*

The rain stopped. Sudden silence. The sky was completely black, not a star above. It thundered in the distance like God approved of my acceptance.

I lost my balance and fell into the shallow surf. A wave pushed over my face. Fetter gargled in and out of detail as the tide pushed and receded. The water flowed into me and through me. Fetter bent over, her face close to the water. Her lips moved.

Darling.

Her fingers dipped into the water and penetrated my chest. I felt the breeze on her cheeks. We were no longer separate. I am her, she is me. Exhilaration vibrated inside her/me.

Take me.

Balance returned to the world. Water gushed through me like fresh air. My mind dissolved in the vast ocean. And it felt good. Felt right. Fetter's love was warm and embracing. I will be happy here.

As I integrated further into the world, I began to see in all directions. I saw through Fetter's eyes. She was looking down at me, my face below the water. I also saw through my own eyes. I was looking up at her. Lightning gathered in a knot in the blackened sky. It crept from all directions until it was a ball of electric light directly above us. Fetter sensed it, or perhaps saw it through my eyes. She saw it too late.

Lightning exploded down like a javelin. For a nanosecond, I expected it to pierce through her chest, a bolt from a god striking another god at just the moment of distraction.

It plunged through *my* chest!

The last of my vision caught the look of Fetter's shock. The lightning then took my sight. An enormous vacuum pulled at the hole in my chest, followed by an excruciating sense of expansion.

Bones breaking, flesh tearing.

I sensed the fading of the details around me.

There was silence. Blackness. Emptiness.

Then a flash of blue and the compression of a wormhole.

TRUTH

I remember screaming.

The sensation of bursting. Blood. Sand.

There is a vision of a black, lightless planet. Somehow, I absorbed Fetter. She existed only in the circuits that made up that planet, like an electronic ghost. She is a program, but somehow she is immortal. She didn't need the black planet to exist. And she can't be destroyed. I know this because she's inside me.

The black planet is dead without her. Pivot struck when I integrated with her. For I am not a gift. Not a son.

I am a weapon.

WHEN A DAM BREAKS

I was on my back. Eyes closed.

I felt enormous. Not the fat-bloated-tearing enormous, more like my presence filled the inside of the black ship that had taken me through the wormholes. I felt interconnected with the smooth curvature of the discus-shaped walls. It was half buried in a sand dune.

But I wasn't just expansive and connected with the ship, I was experiencing everything within the ship, like I was interconnected with *all* physical existence. I was the floating dust particles, the bits of debris on the floor, the stray body hair and shed skin cells and the micro-organisms. I was interlaced with the structure of every molecule inside the ship, including the person standing inside it.

Pivot. The grimmets stormed the Outpost for him, they sensed he'd returned. They knew he was inside me. Did they know he created me?

Fetter was no dream. Pike had not poisoned my mind, no matter how strange and hallucinogenic it was. I was back on Earth, and I carried the truth of my true nature. *I'm not human.*

It's strange to realize your entire life has been a lie. That, in fact, I'm nothing more than circuits and fluid, that my brain is a processor that thinks and believes it's alive, that my memories are just data. That when I die, it won't matter. Not really.

I sat up, opened my eyes. Pivot was there, fourteen feet away in the sunny portion of the invisible-walled ship, just as I knew he was.

My hands looked slightly different. I wiggled my fingers. The ones that were cut off and regenerated, the new ones, were a lighter color than the original skin on my other hand. Long bleached lines ran down my arms like they had split open and new flesh filled in. I pulled up my shirt. My chest was striped, too. There was as much new skin as there was original. I exploded. But the king's men put me back together again. The king, standing in the sun, waiting for me to awaken.

I got up, gingerly. Pain sliced through my earlobe. I expected blood to be on my fingers but the ache faded when I reached for my ear. I stepped to the line of sunlight that cut across the middle of the ship. I remained in the shadow of the sand dune.

[You could not know your true nature.] Pivot's thought resonated in my head. *[You never would've reached Fetter if you had. That is something you couldn't hide.]*

My lips curled over my teeth. "Why?"

[You absorbed all of her and brought us back. Fetter is now here.] He took his hands from behind him, displayed a black cube. It absorbed the sunlight, bending the space around it, appeared more like a square hole in space than an actual object, its mass pulling light back to it. *[Her existence needs to end.]*

Waves of warm, healing energy emanated from him. I didn't want an apology or sympathy. I wanted fucking answers. "You... *created* me. You built me to carry you to her so you could... get revenge? This is about fucking payback?"

[It is about all of life.]

"Don't hand me that shit! I'm talking about what you did to me! You built me!"

[You were born.]

"No, I was *built*. You say it, Pivot. I wasn't born, I was manufactured. Say it."

Silence hardened between us.

"SPEAK TO ME, GODDAMN YOU! Look up and speak to me! You tell me why you did this! You tell me how any creature in this universe deserves this! You tell me how you can live with yourself, how you could build and love a... a..."

Thing. I'm a thing.

For the last year, I felt Pivot near me. Always sensed his presence, his warmth and caring. I had no father; I psychologically craved someone to take his place. Pivot was that presence, he filled that need. I looked for his acceptance and guidance; I followed his footsteps because I believed in him. Was that the plan, to be a father-figure so I would follow him? For that to happen, my father had to be dead.

"You killed him."

[I did not.]

"You tell the truth, did you murder him?"

[Your father was a beautiful man.]

"But it wasn't a bad thing he died. How I had this enormous emotional hole for a father, someone to look up to, and there you were. Was that a coincidence? Because none of this is random, Pivot. This is all one big fucking master plan and Pike knew this. How did he know, Pivot? How did Pike know this was going to happen? Is he part of this, too?"

Pivot didn't respond.

"You're behind it all; you've been steering me like a mule. I'm just bait, dangling on a hook for Fetter to snap up. Well, now the puppet knows he's a puppet. What now?"

[The universe is lucky to have you.]

"SHUT UP WITH THAT!" The ship shuddered. "The universe is no luckier to have me than a rock or a hammer, so I don't want to hear about love and the rest of your lies. That's for humans, Pivot. That's for things that *exist*, that are real. That matter." Sand trickled down the dune. "Not self-aware *things*."

[You do not understand—]

"I understand the only reason I exist was to carry you into Fetter. There's nothing else to understand, no other reason for my life! YOU USED ME!" *Boom. Boom. Boom.* Anger thundered from my chest, thudding against the walls. "How could you do this to me?"

He only stood there, head down, allowing my energy to pound the ship. My presence wrapped around him. The air became my body and I felt his entire being. I latched onto every cell in his body. I could throw him through the wall, crush him into powder, dissect him like a high school science project. But I did none of that. I only forced him to look up. With a thought, I pushed his chin up. His hair fell off his face, exposed an expression of remorse.

"Speak."

[I lost the ability to speak.] He shook the hair from his eyes. *[And see.]*

"Why?"

[Some things cannot be undone.]

"So it's true, what Fetter said. You and her are… you think you're gods?"

[No longer.]

"But you're not real, any more than me."

[Fetter and I created the black planet, but I realized the folly of our existence. I escaped in order to correct my error.]

"You want to destroy her?"

[The time has come.]

"What gives you the right?" The ship creaked under pressure. I took a deep breath, let my pain and confusion penetrate his awareness so that he could feel what he had done.

"What's it like to be so callus, so unfeeling? To behave like a machine?"

[I have not lied to you.]

122

"Have not lied?" Sand slid over the top of the craft, trickling along the side, casting a flowing shadow over the floor. "Your concept of honesty is warped."

[If you knew your true nature, Fetter never would've taken you inside, never would've opened to you, merged with you, allowed you to absorb her. To trap her.]

I charged into the sunlight. *"YOU LET ME LOVE!"*

His eyes moved, but did not focus. His lips parted, but there were no words. Only a thought. *[I have much to atone for.]*

I spit on him. "Manumit is your name."

[I accept that.]

"You are nothing. Pivot is dead."

[I understand.]

"You couldn't possibly. No one in existence could understand what this feels like." I grabbed his face with one hand. "I don't want to know why you did this because I don't care about your petty war. I loved you. *How* could you do this to me? That's what I don't understand. How could you do this to anyone?"

He opened his mind, thoughts drifted toward me. Images of his past. Effortlessly, and spitefully, I pushed them away. "Don't touch me with your mind." I stepped closer, he could feel my breath. "Just explain."

[If you wish to understand, you must see.]

His milky eyes looked directly at me. His thoughts waited. He would not force them on me. In fact, he couldn't force me to do anything. I had become more than him. I walked away, feeling anger seethe like a pyre. My presence pushed against the confines of the ship. The walls buckled. I didn't want his touch, didn't want his presence. But I wanted to know.

I walked to the back of the ship where it was dark, trembling. When all was still, I opened my mind. Visions of his past drifted toward me and melted into my consciousness. I closed my eyes.

I saw his life.

[My ancestors were pioneers.]

123

The space craft was the size of a stadium and sparkled with lights where people lived normal lives. It was large enough to grow crops and raise animals, everything to sustain life. The ship travelled through thousands of solar systems by finding natural wormholes in space.

Eventually, they uncovered the secret to space and existed in a vacuum of time that moved sideways instead of forward. Many generations were born and raised on that ship before those on their home planet aged a second in time.

[Their mission was to find a habitable planet besides their own. It became their only mission. However, they had become lost and, despite their navigational technology, they could not find their way back home.]

The ship hovered past planet after planet, some with water and ice while others were hot and dry. When the conditions were deemed habitable, they transported to the surface. But the environments were still harsh where wind punished igloo-shaped buildings under a sulfuric yellow sky. Scientists studied data, hoping they could find a way to survive without the aid of suits and equipment, hoping that one day they could leave the ship.

Instead, each planet brought sickness and death.

[My people discovered so many solar systems, but so many were lost and so little was learned. They simply couldn't adapt to another planet. They were destined to remain on a decaying ship. Hope faded. Until I was born.]

On board the ship, a child ran through the corridors, chased by older kids. This boy had sandy hair. His eyes were clear blue. The kids caught this child and even though they were bigger, he deftly avoided their clutches, striking at their knees and slipping between their legs until he escaped.

This child was eighteen when he took command of the deep space colony. The population had dwindled and there were few left to challenge him, but it wouldn't have mattered. Some men are trained to lead. Others are born. His visage was calm yet demanding. He was reliable, always at his post. He led all explorations. When they returned, he personally went to each family to express his sorrow for their loss. Afterwards, he sought quietude with a woman.

As the years went by, they had a daughter. Some nights, he watched his family sleep. And some nights, the captain silently wept. He wasn't supposed to be weak; he was expected to embody strength and fearlessness. But his people were running out of time.

Even heroes falter.

[There was a choice to be made: watch my people die or embrace technology. After generations of searching, it was clear we would never be able to adapt to another planet. Our bodies were organic. Vulnerable. If I chose technology, we could survive. But there would be no turning back. In my mind, the choice was simple.]

The captain was in a laboratory, strapped onto a white bed, his head secured with steel bands. A crew of scientists watched from behind a glass wall. His wife was among them. She did not chew on her fingernails or tap her foot, for she was the wife of the captain, and his duty included risk.

Stainless steel infusion guns fit through holes on the bed, pressed against his spine, a barrel for each vertebra. The captain clenched the white sheet. He took three short breaths, held the last one and blinked. A green light turned on.

He tried not to scream.

[I was the first to accept the conversion into inorganic existence. It was controversial technology, but we had experimented with rats. We did not know if it would work on a human, but I'd seen enough of my people die.]

He shook long after the infusion guns were removed and the green light turned off. The scientists watched him convulse. Spittle foamed on his lips and he broke through the steel straps. The captain fell on the floor. The scientists rushed in to help, but there was nothing they could do.

[The nanomechs imitated blood cells and began the replication of the body's organs, muscles and blood. If we were

correct, my organic body would be replaced with an exact duplication of mechanized cells. Like a full body prosthesis.]

The captain lay in a coma for weeks with his wife by his side. They monitored his vitals and watched his heart beat slower and blood pressure drop. Even when his heart stopped beating and began to hum, he was still alive.

Conversion complete.

[I awoke a new man, no longer organic. No longer human. But I had the same memories. The same personality.]

On a mountainous planet where precipitation hissed like acid on an igloo hut, the captain stepped outside. The scientists followed in protective suits. He raised his arms, laughing loudly in the howling wind. The rain melted his skin, but it just as quickly healed.

[I became indestructible.]

The lab was expanded with more beds and infusion guns. Conversion technology was in full swing and the people lined up. The infusions healed their bodies. There was no difference in how they felt or behaved, they only felt better. Even the children were converted and continued to grow and mature, some without a clue of what they had become.

[Not all conversions were successful. Some bodies rejected the nanomechs like a virus. We all made sacrifices to survive. I was no different.]

The captain held his wife's hand just before their child was pushed away on a rolling bed. They stood at the glass wall and watched the infusion guns pump the nanomechs into her. Watched her flail about. Watched the monitors flat-line. The scientists did everything they could to revive her. The captain and his wife pushed them away, furiously thumped her chest. In the end, they held her, rocking back and forth. They buried her alone, on an unknown planet, dug the hole with their bare hands.

[For the survivors, our intelligence was efficient and flawless, we thought at tremendous speeds. Our activity could operate at the speed of light. And we spread throughout the known universe.]

Planets passed, each of various colors and sizes orbiting different stars. Exploratory shuttles were launched and the pioneers walked onto the surface of each planet, regardless of weather and atmosphere. Images of dinosaurs and human-like beings and curious apes flashed through my vision, exhibiting countless habitable climates they discovered as they travelled sideways in time.

[We learned to merge our minds and think collectively, formulating theories never before possible. We discovered realms of existence never dreamed of. Parallel universes. Ethereal worlds.]

Many of them meditated, all facing the wall. They began to vibrate. Apparitions of their bodies floated toward the center of the room and merged. Then I saw the deep space ship split into two images, as if it copied itself in space, and went in opposite directions, through different wormholes. Colors, shapes and sounds warped the image, flashing and twisting in strange patterns.

[We became all things. All powerful. God-like.]

The colors merged to form a close-up of a large blue eye.

[But in time, we grew colder.]

The view backed out, revealed the captain's ashen face. Hard and cold.

[The price of our immortality was our humanity. We forgot what we are. We were void of a soul. Hungry ghosts.]

The view backed further out. The captain stood stolid on an icy tundra, sleet spitting sideways across frozen desolation.

[We were without essence: the life-giving presence of our being. We craved existence.]

The view pulled further out. Bodies were on the ice, lying in contorted poses. As the view continued back, the bodies of humans extended on and on, scattered through the wasteland.

[So we took it from others.]

Manumit and Fetter walked hand-in-hand down a city sidewalk, one that could easily pass for New York. People fell in their wake, their essence floated from them like silky fog,

127

absorbed into their bodies. There was panic in the streets. They took their time; there was no hurry. All they had was time.

The landscapes changed, sometimes they were in the countryside and the captain and his wife would sit with families to break bread, afterwards sneak into their room like a vampire. Sometimes centuries would pass on a populated planet, but it was always left barren of life.

[We fed like parasites, but satisfaction was so short-lived and we became hungrier. Greedier. Worlds suffered, greatly.]

Mortars exploded and jets sizzled overhead dropping death from the sky. Tanks and rocket propelled grenades exploded around Manumit, but he was unfazed, instantly healing and continuing his death crusade. Planet after planet.

[Humans detested us, prayed that their gods abandoned them to the devil. We could consume a planet in months. We grew hungrier, still, and I was weary of the chase. Instead, I used our technology to build a home.]

The black planet was dense and lifeless, absorbing light. It was a vessel of artificiality. But inside were green hills and sultry sunsets. Water fell from the side of the mountain face, spilling into the lake below, sending a rainbow arching over the mist.

[I convinced the others to follow us. But when they arrived, Fetter and I absorbed their stolen essence and ate what was left of them. We only needed each other. And when the desire for essence howled inside us again, we ventured out to another planet.]

Billions of bluish tendrils extended from the black planet, extending out into space like glowing roots. These wormholes led to life, somewhere in existence, connecting everything to the black planet and siphoned the essence of all that lived.

A cancer cell.

[We were soul-eaters, and our victims gave their essence, their experience and life. Until we sucked the entire planet dry.]

Cities were empty. Weeds sprouted among the dilapidated high rises. Cars rusted in driveways and airplanes were buried in snow.

[No human stood a chance.]

The thoughts and images receded. I opened my eyes and observed him, over my shoulder. His head was bowed again, the cube cradled in his hands. The sun had moved across the sky and the line of sunlight was creeping deeper into the shade.

[We knew we were not alive, that we had become a disease, but we ignored it. We were gods. Our will was undeniable. Nothing in the universe could stop us, until we encountered a seemingly innocent species.]

Another image appeared in my mind, this one of a blue planet, similar to the countless ones that had been drained of life.

[The grimmets were creatures we never knew existed. They contained this amazing intelligence and beamed with an intensity of essential life like no other. They were immune to us, but they could not stop us from sucking the rest of the planet of life.]

The image of a vibrant, thriving environment quickly dried up. Plants shriveled. Skeletons littered the landscape. Dust blew over the red mountains where the Grimmet Outpost now sat on the lifeless planet.

The grimmets sat on the limbs of dead trees watching a man and a woman walk across the deserted plains, preparing to return to the black planet. Fetter was the first to dissolve into the air like a figure of sand, followed by a blue flash in the gray sky. But Manumit turned and looked over his shoulder. The grimmets caught his attention.

[Before we were finished, the grimmet species left me with a thought.]

His eyes narrowed.

[They gave me the answer.]

His posture softened. He looked over the world he'd just decimated like he was seeing it for the first time. He saw what he'd done.

[They showed me home.]

I saw the image they had put in Manumit's mind. I saw a planet that was blue and green. I saw forests and buildings, rivers and oceans and deserts. And I saw the people there. I recognized this planet.

"Earth?" I turned and walked toward him. "How could this be your home?"

[The Paladins launched the space program to find life in the universe. The original space pioneers traveled sideways in time while Earth had barely aged. For my people, eons passed.]

"The original space pioneers… they're *Paladins?*"

He bowed his head.

"They created you."

[They could not foresee the events that led to our creation.]

"But, how could they not know?"

[We were lost, how could they?]

It was true. As powerful as the Paladin Nation was, they were nothing compared to the secrets of the universe. How could they know they'd created the black planet? How could they know they were responsible for a cosmic disease?

[After the grimmets, I returned to the black planet, but what they showed me would not fade. I began to remember my original face.]

I saw the child run down the corridor.

[At first, I considered erasing the memory like corrupt data, but the longer I held it, the more pressing it became. The compulsion to remember my original self was too great. I knew there was an end to our ceaseless journey, our unending thirst, in remembering our true nature. I knew the black planet would have to end. Fetter, though, was not convinced.]

"You're human, again?"

[No.] He turned his head, slightly, self-conscious of his dead eyes. *[But there is hope.]*

"You think you're going to heaven?"

[I don't know where I'm going.]

"You betrayed me."

[As I've said, there is much to atone.]

Anger twisted inside me, the currents punching dents in the invisible walls of the ship, warping bubbles in space. The ship wailed, shifting in the dune and tilting toward Pivot.

"So you wanted to save the day, but needed to bait the hook, so why not me? I'm not real, not a person. I'm inorganic, just like her. Throw me in front of the runaway train."

[You did something no other being could do.]

"I'm a machine."

[No machine could do what you did. It is your ability to love, to open and become vulnerable, that allowed you to do so. You are very human.]

I lifted my hand, displayed the new fingers, lifted my shirt, revealed the stripes of new flesh. Not flesh. Nanomechs pretending to be flesh, pretending to be everything that was me: my thoughts, my mind, heart, all just a script.

"You call this human?"

[I spent eons in seclusion, searching for the right human to carry forth my plan. In all the universe, you are that person.]

"STOP SAYNG THAT, GODDAMN YOU! I'm not a person!"

[You were cloned from a person.]

"Then use him!"

[Because no human could withstand the pain and suffering that you have endured. No machine could, either. You are the machine that became human.]

"The machine that *thinks* it's human."

[You have a mother—]

"I DON'T HAVE A MOTHER!"

[— that loves you very much.]

"Tell that to my clone."

[It is not the human race that needs you. It is all of life.]

He raised the cube, as if the responsibility was mine. I slapped it out of his hands and punctured the wall. A hissing stream of compressed air shot into the desert. Pain sliced my earlobe again as the cube bounced over the floor.

I shielded my eyes from the sunlight, picked up the cube. It was impossibly heavy to lift. It was only my telekinetic ability that allowed me to hold it in my palm where it gyrated with low frequency. It contained a god.

My earlobe buzzed again.

"I wish you luck," I said. "Heaven's filled with a lot of pissed off people." I placed the cube in Pivot's hands. "Hell, too."

[Please, understand.]

I walked around, felt the smooth walls of the ship with my mind. I put my finger through the hole. It was time to stretch out. I had been contained long enough. As easy as striking out with my fist, I willed to be free.

The side of the ship exploded.

The ground thundered.

Black shrapnel from the ship's wall fell from the sky, slicing into the sand hundreds of yards away. The heat of the desert whooshed into the ship. I stood at the jagged edge, the sand several feet below. The air dried my nostrils and my physical presence soared over the dunes, sprung from the ship like a failed dam. I merged with each particle of sand, merged with the lichens surviving on the stones, the scorpions and spiders and snakes and cacti, the jackrabbits and lizards and coyotes. I felt it all. Connected with them. Became them.

The sand crunched between my boot and floor. Pivot gently touched my arm.

[I can only isolate Fetter for a period of time. The data needs to be reconfigured and returned to the black planet to shut down all systems. If she escapes, Earth will be next. I have risked much for this moment.]

"And you need me to take her back?"

[I require your assistance.]

I sucked the hot air through my nostrils, looked thoughtfully into the barren desert. "You wanted a machine to be human, Pivot. So I'll act human. Flawed and self-centered."

[You are the only hope.]

"Then you failed."

I took the first step off the ship, landing softly in the sand. Into the desert I walked. Pivot remained in the ship, still and silent. He had said all that needed to be said. And I had listened.

What else could he do?

Nothing.

CHILD OF FETTER

It was such a relief when I stepped out of the ship. My telekinetic presence pushed outward like a star. I connected with all the Mojave Desert. The ecosystem and organisms in it remained separate, their own existence, but I felt their movement, their compulsion, hunger and pain and pleasure.

I stopped at the top of the nearest dune. Desolation was as far as I could see, but the desert teamed with life at the cellular level. My presence continued to expand, crawling across the desert, its reach going farther and farther, knowing and becoming the physical world for several miles. Fetter had changed me, stretched my senses beyond the limitations of human existence. I was now like the universe, expanding outward. Becoming everything.

The sun was still overhead, but I didn't feel it. I was utilizing and storing the sunlight, converting its heat into energy. The universe had the potential for endless giving. I was channeling that energy into my being.

I sliced time, speeding my metabolism at the cellular level. The sun stuck above me and the slight breeze died in the stillness of earth's frozen moment. The world would not resume their lives while I walked the desert. I needed it to be still for a while. It would be a long walk.

I willed the sand to whirl in front of me, blowing out of the way and forming a flat path. There was a time I pondered the purpose of life. I didn't like pain. I didn't like emptiness, couldn't understand why anyone would exist to suffer, it wasn't rational. Why try? Could I just get my life over with? We all had to end, so what's the point of suffering until then? When I discovered my Paladin powers, I understood the inseparable oneness of us all, the immortal existence of the present moment, how each life was precious and that I could help others understand that truth for themselves. That with understanding, all people could find peace, experience the pure joy of their existence.

But I'm nothing like them. I'm just a signpost, an image, a reflection of their potential. Just a program.

I willed the dunes to flatten out before me. I uprooted scrub and rolled away boulders with a flicker of thought, walking straight across the endless desert. I walked for miles, and in all that time the sun did not move. My body did not exhaust in the timeslice. Not only was I drawing on the sun's energy, I was taking it from the life around me – the insects and snakes and rodents – as they became part of my existence, connecting telekinetically with my body. I took from their mitochondria. I took from the atoms that constructed their being, from the magnetic balance of protons and electrons, took from the neutrinos, up quarks and down quarks. I took essence.

I am a child of Fetter. The black planet.

So be it.

And with the endless supply of essence, the secrets of the universe unfolded in my mind. I saw the fabric of space-time, how time was simply a direction of space. How the interconnection of all life was dimensional fabric that could be traversed in any direction like the flatness of the desert plain.

I saw my life spread out in this fabric, sensing each moment, each memory like a byte of data, all connected like a string that made up Socket Greeny, dangling behind me. And the future was a vaporized bit of existence coming together as I chose my path. Where would it lead? Was it already predetermined? Did Pivot draw my life in the fabric of space-time like a stick in sand and set me loose like a mechanical mouse, trained to go where it was supposed to go? And while the desert crunched under me, I saw the very beginning of my life, when it first started. The moment of birth.

Pressure on my head. Pushing from behind and then viscous sliding.

My chest inflates.

Images blur in front of me. A single face. The details are blurry, but Pivot's presence is unmistakable. I feel it in my core, know its love.

I am born.

Suddenly, there is a tremendous sensation of separation. I am missing something, pulled away from a presence that I have always known. Something I have always been.

And now it is gone.

Born? Could that be my clone, my original self's memory? Could that be what I have always felt was missing, the presence of my original self? Even at birth, I knew my essential self was somewhere else. I didn't feel real. Because I'm not. I was just an imitation.

There is much discomfort as I grow. Hunger, ear infections, exhaustion. I learn to cope. And, often, I find comfort in the faces of my mother and father, looking down on me in the crib, in the car seat, sometimes stern, sometimes joyous, but always supportive. Always loving.

I am always with them.

I'm sitting on my father's lap as Fourth of July fireworks light up the sky. Mother is laughing somewhere. Later, I put on his boots that rattle on my tiny feet. I am looking down a flight of steps and the world tumbles. The bottom step hits hard on the back of my head. I feel Pivot's presence as I draw in the first long breath to bellow the alarming cry. He does not help, but he is there as my mother and father arrive, carry me back inside the house. I can feel him.

I couldn't see Pivot, but he has always been there. He has always managed to avoid being seen, to be anywhere he wanted. To follow and watch. Did he shove me down the steps, just so I could experience life's pain?

I am five, watching television. Mother is letting me watch television when I should be in bed, but she's in her bedroom crying. I knock on the door, to ask if she's all right, but she's talking to someone. I don't hear anyone answer, and she's barely able to make sense, her words are garbled in sobs. I don't know who's with her, but I sense it's someone familiar, but it's not my father.

My babysitter stays with me the next day. And then Mother tells me about Father. She tells me he's not coming home anymore. I'm confused. Why won't he come home?

Because God took him, she says.

Why would he do that?

From then on, the emotional hole was bigger than ever. I was born with something missing, and now it was as deep as the ocean. The joy of life was gone. Mother didn't smile. Father's boots weren't around. And the emptiness consumed me, until I didn't smile, either.

"*I don't think about them, much,*" Streeter says. "*But I wish they were here.*"

We're seven, climbing into his treehouse to look at magazines.

"*At least you got your gramma and grampa,*" I say.

"*Yeah, but their Christmas presents suck.*"

"*That's why you want your parents back? Better presents?*"

He laughs, but his attempt to avoid the emptiness in his being fails. He nervously lifts the magazine, then shows me a cool skateboard ramp for the backyard. His emptiness resonates in my stomach.

Streeter never spoke about his parents again, at least not until we were older. He didn't know how to deal with it, except ignore it.

Chute was different.

"You like that?" I say.

Chute is in the gift shop. We're in sixth grade, on a field trip. She's looking at a plastic recorder instrument, something we had to play in grade school to learn music. We hated it and swore we'd never play it, again. But there she was, stroking the holes.

"I was just remembering that my mom liked it," she says. "She used to dance with my sister when I played."

"She danced to Hot Cross Buns?"

"It didn't matter what I played."

When she's not looking, I buy it and give it to her on the bus. She doesn't say much. Later, she plays a song and Streeter and I dance.

Chute's emptiness was open and hurtful, but unlike Streeter, she let it be there. She let it be part of her. It felt like falling in a hole that had no bottom, but Chute let that happen because she didn't want to forget her mother, no matter how much it hurt. I didn't understand that, not then.

I'd known death and loss forever. Was that why we were so close?

We wait at the bus stop. It's the first day of school. Streeter's gramma comes out with a camera and takes the picture that Chute still has on her wall. And there, lurking in the back, the familiar presence. The presence I had known all my life. Something inseparable from my life, something I didn't even notice. Someone was always there.

Watching.

Pivot. He was the blur in the picture. Watching, guiding, following. Building his plan, making sure I felt human. I remembered how it felt to be human. I remembered pain, I knew death and joy and love.

Always there.

139

"GODDAMN YOU!" My rage burst in a seismic wave, uprooting every plant within miles, tossing boulders in the air and flipping cacti headfirst into the sand. I couldn't feel Pivot, he was no longer in the desert. I stretched my presence for miles, felt all the way back to the shipwreck. The ship was gone. I extended my influence farther, but he was gone.

Was any of it real? Did he manipulate everything so that I would be friends with the right people, have the despondent mother and the brainy friend and the girlfriend I would fall in love with so that I experienced sadness and joy and loss and fullness, so that his creation would appear human enough to trap Fetter? Is that what my life was, a fucking game?

Pain defines us. Reminds us we're human.

Pike told me that. He knew about papa Pivot. He knew this day was coming. How could he? And what else did he know?

I stopped walking. Without my footsteps, the desert was dead silent. Destruction lay all around. The plants would soon dry out. Insects would be buried. I put things back in order, moving everything within my connected presence. The desert reassembled itself before me. It would live again, just as it had before I froze time. No one would even notice I walked through the desert. I would be invisible; the only proof would be the string of my existence on the fabric of time.

Space and time are inseparable.

And if I can manipulate time, I can manipulate space.

I closed my eyes, spreading out to the far reaches of the desert, to the foot of the mountains many miles away. Every molecule, each atom, resonated with my being. I was a body, but was inseparable from the essence of life. And if I wished, if I willed it to be so, I could transfer my body through the atoms of space to the outer reaches of my influence, transferring my physical existence like a sound wave passes through air, like a wave rolls across the ocean.

My body seemed less solid, the barrier of my skin becoming gray and fuzzy as it dissolved into the atoms. Thinner I became until my awareness blew in the atmosphere like a dust cloud. I

140

floated with the cloud of my body, all the way to the foot of the mountain range where the dust cloud of my atoms reassembled and condensed. My organs solidified and my skin tightened.

I opened my eyes.

The shadow of the mountain fell over me. I'd traversed several miles within seconds.

I expanded outward, again, pushing through the solid mountains, connecting with the inner core of sand and miniscule algae and delicate lichens, past the reaches of the desert into the town on the other side where I merged with houses and cars and people, absorbing their memories and desires and worries.

I can go anywhere. Be anything.

Pike was calling me, I could feel it.

I closed my eyes, felt the dissolution of my body. Somehow I knew I would find him in South Carolina.

III

Your entire life may prepare you for one moment,
a single second in time that means everything.
When that moment arrives, will you be there?
Pivot

Let go over a cliff, die completely, and then come back to life.
After that you cannot be deceived.
Buddhist proverb

I have seen the beginning and end of the universe.
Do you want the answer?
Pick up a cup and drink from it.
Do so purely, without thought.
That is the face of God.
Socket

HEARTS THAT HUM

South Carolina was a thousand miles away.

I crossed the land, one enormous leap at a time. Cars that were once speeding along were frozen to the concrete like a wax museum. The passengers appeared to be singing or facially numb with boredom.

I crossed through Kentucky and Tennessee, stopping often to admire the countryside and the horses in their gated land, lips to the turf. I floated over the top of the Smokey Mountains, walking along the curving Interstate, towing the dashed line between massive trucks and tiny cars. I stepped off the Blue Ridge Mountains and dissolved before hitting the trees, merging with the green foliage and crumbled bedrock.

I walked through Columbia. My heart was barely thumping anymore. By the time I reached Charleston, it started to hum.

I needed to find Pike.

My physical expansion spread out over the Lowcountry of South Carolina, reaching into the outer limits of Charleston, merging with the wetlands and egrets and brackish water. I focused, feeling everything in existence between my body and my destination and, with a thought, relaxed into the ether and felt my body dissolve one more time.

I came together in front of the high school. The front doors were open, students were frozen in mid-stride. School was out.

I solidified inside the grassy circle of the turnabout where buses were lined up. Three flagpoles were behind me. The flags were swept in a non-existent breeze, as if molded from bronze.

The sun was partially obscured by broken clouds. There was no way to measure the amount of time I spent in the timeslice, but I had grown accustomed to the sound of my breath and footsteps, absent was the sounds of daily living. *Did I even need to breathe?*

Slowly, the fragrance of grass and the sounds of people intensified as I returned to normal time and molecules began to drift. The flags snapped overhead and the first bus in line began to creep ahead. Shouts and playful screaming started slow and came to full speed as my body synchronized with Earth's regular time and those that lived in it.

Hundreds of students fled for freedom, racing into the parking lots, their thoughts a random collage of desires and fears, locked into their identities of geeks or jocks or queens or studs, gearheads, burners, gamers or flamers. I felt their lungs expand and vocal chords vibrate. I absorbed their concerns about parties and clubs, who was doing what and who was dating who. I was a distant shadow that tasted their experiences and absorbed the essence that was their life.

The natural tendency to steal their essence was suddenly repulsive. I may not be human, but I wouldn't become Fetter. I had to stop.

In the mix of it all, a pair of girls came out to the flagpoles and began winding down the flags. Shannon Quigley and Stacy Parker, they'd been best friends since second grade, spending the night with each other almost every weekend. Right now, Stacy wanted Charlie Nelson to ask her to prom and Shannon was secretly jealous, hoping he wouldn't but telling Stacy something supportive because that's what best friends do. But if she got a date—

I snapped back. I was already siphoning their essence again, along with their thoughts and memories.

They lowered the flags, not a foot away from me. They didn't notice me or my shadow next to theirs. They were folding the flags and on the topic of homework when I felt Chute. She was on the second floor, coming down the steps with two friends, holding her books to her chest. She slowed down as she approached the bottleneck at the front doors, past the security guards.

There she is.

She lit up the yard like another sun, her essence beaming brightly, sinking warmly into my chest. My fading heartbeat quickened, as if remembering what it once was.

She laughed at something Suzy Keller on her left said, then looked at Jonie White on her right. Chute's ponytail whipped from one shoulder to the next. They stopped at the curb and looked both directions. The buses were loaded and gone. Cars honked and Denny Stillbee hung out the window of his car. Chute and the girls laughed. I felt her joy inside me. And as the yard cleared, I watched her walk with her friends to the parking lot. Suzy was going to take her home. Cars passed between us. She was almost out of sight. I was going to let her go. But then she stopped.

My chest thumped.

She tipped her head, unsure of what she saw. It was what she felt that made her turn around and look. She shaded her eyes, searching. I don't remember becoming visible, but somehow she saw me. She called over her shoulder to Suzy to hang on a second, she'd be right back. When she crossed the roundabout road, she ran.

She jumped into my arms. I tightened, afraid she would see me for what I was. But her essence was so intoxicating; I forgot for an instant that my world had imploded.

"Are you picking me up?" she asked.

I put her down and she grabbed my hand. I backed up but she pulled my hand to her. It must've been the look on my face that changed the energetic colors around her. Her essence suddenly contracted and soured.

"Are you all right?" she asked.

I lightly jerked my hand from her grip, hiding the new fingers behind my back like it was all the evidence she needed. The slashing weapon. Fingers falling.

LIAR.

I backed up a step.

"Why are you acting so weird?" she asked. "Did I do something?"

"No." I took her with my other hand. "You didn't do... everything's all right. I'm just a little tired, that's all."

"Well, what're you doing here?"

"I just wanted to see you. And talk to Streeter."

"He's in the virtualmode lab, as usual." She pointed at the front doors. "You'll have to call him, security won't let you back in the school."

Amanda Flenner shouted at Chute, said something about leading the student cabinet meeting next week. Chute hollered back. Her complexion was so fair, the freckles highlighted on her smooth cheeks. The skin crinkled between her eyes when she laughed.

She reached out without turning while talking to Amanda and hooked her finger with mine. I stared at our hands, recalling the vision of when we were older. *Not all visions come true.*

"So, are you taking me to the Garrison?" she said, swinging our hands back and forth.

"What?"

"I'm going to play tagghet with the kids today, remember? Spindle was going to pick me up at my house, he didn't think you'd be back yet." She shrugged, girlishly. "I'm so happy you're back."

"I, uh, no I forgot. I'm sorry, I just went through a lot today, there's a lot on my mind."

"Did your meeting go bad?"

"It wasn't good."

"I'm sorry. Maybe we can go out and cheer you up. I was talking to Janette and she wants the four of us to go out. We could do it tomorrow!"

Suzy pulled through the roundabout and honked, looked at Chute strangely and said, "What're you doing, talking to flagpoles?"

"Oh, that's not nice," Chute said, not getting it.

"I got to go, I don't want to be late," she said. "Will you be at the Garrison later? I want to play with the grimmets and they're always more fun when you're around."

"Maybe," I said.

She kissed me on the corner of my mouth and frowned. "Are you sure you're all right? You're so cold."

I nodded and kissed her back.

Then watched her go.

It hurt when she left. The beating faded in my chest. The hum grew louder.

NO MASK

"I just need to go to the office, man." It was Jake Studard, starting left tackle for the football team. He was trying to shoulder his way past the security guard. "Just call the coach, he'll explain."

"You call the coach." The security guard played the same position ten years earlier, now he had three kids and a wife and a bit of a drinking problem. He wasn't budging. "It ain't my problem. Once you're out of the building, you stay out."

The security guard hooked his thumb in his belt. I slipped past him just as he stopped Meg Chansey with the crazy idea she could get back inside because she was class president.

The hallways were mostly empty. A few students hanging out at their lockers and a small group of teachers were outside the office. The essence of their experiences drifted into me, charging the hum in my chest. The three of them looked around like a ghost just passed.

I turned the corner and tread up the wide steps to the second floor. No one was within a hundred feet, except at the end of the hall, behind the vault door of the virtualmode lab. Four people were in there. My insatiable essence-hunger fled into the walls and lockers and classrooms, feeding on the memories of past students, their fears and apprehension, the joy of being asked to homecoming by the right guy or the panic of getting one's ass kicked after school. They saturated the wood like blood; buzzed inside me.

The door slid open and Mr. Buxbee walked into the hall, looking over his big round belly at the shiny floor as he semi-waddled toward me. His lower lip plumped out and he hummed a quiet tune, something he always did when few people were around. My favorite virtualmode instructor passed me without looking.

I stopped outside the door and stared at the scanlock where a key could be waved. Not many keys were given out to that room. The gear inside was worth more than the entire school. I could feel the circuits inside the lock and followed them with my mind. I didn't need a key. I simply asked the door to open. And it did.

The room was half the size of a regular classroom and twice as cold to keep the gear from overheating. Workbenches lined the walls. A large silver table was centered in the middle. Streeter and Janette stood on each side of it, staring at the half-spherical black object, their hands pressed flat on the table, mumbling to each other a checklist before they tested the locator again. They didn't look up, consumed with the project at hand, assuming I was Buxbee returning for something he forgot.

Slowly, I allowed them to see me.

"Holy shit!" Streeter stepped back. "How'd you... when did you get here?"

"My meeting ended." My voice was eerily quiet.

He came over, hand out, and slapped it into mine, clasping his other hand over it and shaking. I automatically felt a connection with him. He felt a tug in his belly. I let go of him before I started sipping on his essence, but not before he shook his head, a little dizzy, not sure what just happened.

"I need a favor," I said.

"All you got to do is ask." He stepped back, rubbing his stomach. "Give me a second, I'll get the technician started on a setup."

Buxbee's assistant, Peter Hammel, had a college degree in networking and virtualmode world building. And Streeter was telling him what to do. Peter didn't seem to mind. Janette was listening, making sure she understood what they were doing.

I wandered to the wall where a shelf displayed several awards. Five of them recognized the school's exceptional development of virtualmode training and execution, which was primarily because of Buxbee, but two had Streeter's name. The larger of the two awards was a three-dimensional prism. I took it down, the colors switching through the transparent surface. *State Champion Codebreaker.* Best high school codebreaker in South Carolina. Did he know his endless potential?

"He talks about you all the time." Janette stared at the glittering trophy. "Socket this, Socket that. I wish he would talk about me the way he talks about you."

I looked into the award like it contained the lifetime of memories with Streeter, each one more entertaining then the next. I wish I could put those memories inside her so that she could feel the same joy.

"What's so funny?" she asked.

I didn't realize I was grinning, so I shared a memory with her. I told her when we were in kindergarten, we stayed the night at each other's house so much that we each had our favorite cereal at each house. We'd be buried behind our box on each side of the table, slurping milk and reading the back of the box for the hundredth time. I was a Corn Pops kid. He was Fruity Pebbles.

"I'm glad you're around to keep an eye on him," I said.

"Why? Where are you going?"

I took a long breath. "I'm not sure."

We stared at the awards for a while longer, then she tugged me away to the table and told me about their progress with the locator. It was on a little stand. Their appointment with NASA was only a week away and, aside from when it screwed up with me, it had been operating flawlessly. It could also mean a lot of money. She opened a holographic circuitry layout that stretched over the table.

"What's up?" Streeter walked up.

"Just showing Socket the locator plans."

"Socket could figure this stuff out in his head," Streeter said. "You wouldn't believe what he can do."

Neither would you.

"So what's the favor?" Streeter asked.

"I'm sorry, Janette, but can I speak to Streeter alone?"

"Yeah, oh, sure... I can, I'll just be... I'll go—"

"If you want to help Peter, I'm not sure he fully understands what I need him to do," Streeter said. "We probably won't be long."

She said goodbye, grabbed her things and left. I paced around the table, thinking where to start. How to start.

"You all right?" Streeter asked.

"I would never ask you for this if it wasn't important."

"Well, what is it? You need money? Help codebreaking?"

"I just need to use the school's virtualmode portal."

"That's it? That's not a big favor."

"I might snap some alarms."

He cocked his head. "What kind of alarms?"

"I'm not sure, but it might get you in trouble."

"I'm always up for trouble." But he drummed his fingers on the table. "Is it that important?"

"I wouldn't ask."

He nodded. And drummed. Then pointed at one of the oversized chairs against the wall. "You can't do anything I can't handle. Have a seat."

"I'll stand."

"All right." He laughed, nervously, then said with a squeaky tone, "Should I be freaking out about now?"

Yes. "I'll explain in a minute."

"That's not helping."

"Sorry."

He considered again. Anyone else in the world and he would've called security. Instead, he sat at the mainframe monitor. "I'll get the transporters ready."

"No need."

He looked over his shoulder. "You still have the imbed transporter in your neck?"

"I'll explain later. Promise."

"Sure." He spun on the seat and crossed his arms. "Then launch when you're ready."

I didn't need the transporters or any sort of gear. In fact, I really didn't need to ask Streeter to use the school's virtualmode portal, but I didn't want to get him in trouble without him knowing. I'd already penetrated the entire lab, followed the circuitry and routers down to the school's portal that powered the virtualmode experience that communicated with millions of portals all over the world like a network of ethereal pipelines, where people existed in virtual reality.

I only needed the portal to access the Internet network so I could spread my influence worldwide, like pouring my consciousness into a system of veins. I wouldn't be able to expand as far without it. I needed to feel everything, searching for the one person that could answer my questions. I moved my awareness through the portal and instantly stretched across the planet, knowing and feeling everything without leaving my body. I closed my eyes, whispering his name.

Pike.

His essence was as unique as his fingerprint. I could distinguish the difference between every person, every machine, everything that was operating on the worldwide virtualmode network. Suddenly, the school's portal contracted.

"Artificial intelligence has breached virtualmode."

I forced it to open back up, sniffing the mental realm like a bloodhound. I was around the world in a second, sensing a strong presence somewhere in a mountainous region. I focused my attention, brought Pike's essence into view, honed in on his location. It was a dead end.

The Garrison.

No way he was in the Garrison. I was sensing the leftover memories of where he spent most of his life. There was little chance I would find him, even with the inexhaustible power I had. The Paladins would have him so secluded that no one could locate him.

I contracted back into my body. Lights were flashing everywhere, along with flickering sounds and high-pitched alarms. The lab door swooshed open and Buxbee and Peter came rushing inside. Streeter was already at the mainframe monitor, shouting that he had it under control. I willed the alarms to quiet and restored the original status of the security. Streeter explained the crossover error of the locator and apologized. He threw the locator in his pocket, promised to work on the coding outside the lab. Buxbee stared at him, then he and Peter turned back to the monitor to assure the integrity.

Streeter grabbed my arm and marched into the hallway. "You want to tell me what's going on?"

LOCATED

I followed Streeter to the elevator, but not before a security guard named Jeff Baker stopped him. "You got a pass?" he asked.

Streeter flashed the badge strung around his neck. "Um, we're going to the library."

The security guard looked around. "Who's we?"

Streeter shrugged.

"Better check in with Mr. Buxbee if you go anywhere else," Jeff said.

We took the elevator up two flights to the top floor. Streeter's leg shook while we waited. We stepped into the circular floor of the library situated on top of the school's tower with windows in all directions. The librarians, still talking in hushed tones even though the floor was empty, looked at Streeter as we exited the elevator. Streeter held up his badge. They went back to talking.

We headed straight for a back room. The windows were wide and clear, overlooking a long wide field stretching out toward the Interstate. The football field was to the left and the tagghet stadium to the right, but between them was a view of the live oaks beyond.

He paced back and forth, muttering to himself while his fingers twittered at his side. It didn't seem like a good idea to tell him the truth, but somehow I owed it to him. Someone should know. I just needed to get it out of me.

"I've known you forever," I said. "You should know this."

"Know what?"

"Have a seat." I pointed at the cushioned chair positioned in front of the window.

"Why? What're you going to do?"

"Just sit down, will you? You don't want to be standing when I show you this."

He sat down, slowly, not taking his eyes off me. "Show me what?"

"Relax, this isn't going to hurt. But it might freak you out a bit."

Tension gripped his body. His muscles were rigid, like I was going to pull a tooth. Lactic acid dumped into his muscles, his body quivered. I had been holding myself tightly wound up, avoided merging with the people around me, avoided siphoning their essence but now I released it, feeling the carpet below my feet, the furniture and dry paper in the books. My awareness exploded outside the window, all the way to the Interstate and the cars speeding toward Charleston.

But I focused on Streeter, his eyes wide open. I willed his body to relax, his mind to open and accept the coming vision. What he saw, what he felt, was the humming in my chest, the regeneration of my fingers and the revelation of my true nature. He saw Pivot tell me I was cloned from a human, that I was created to help him avenge Fetter.

I receded from his consciousness, forced myself to disconnect from the sweet taste of his essence that whirled in my belly. Forced myself not to take from him or anything else within my reach, even though it filled me and tingled inside.

158

His fingers did not nervously twitter. His leg didn't bounce. Instead, he looked at me with a soft expression, then stood, slowly came over and took my hand. He turned it over, studied the back of the light-colored flesh and looked at the palm.

"Are you playing with me?" he asked.

"I wish I were."

He went to the window and leaned his forehead against it. His breath was short. A lightness surged into his experience. His foot slipped off the windowsill and his head began to slide across the glass. I caught him before he fell. It was too much. I should've just told him, giving him a vision was too surreal. Even though he'd known me all his life, saw me when I first sliced time and read thoughts, when I became a Paladin and developed telekinesis, still he was having trouble assimilating this. Even after everything we'd been through, this was a lot.

I placed him in the chair and allowed myself to get inside his mind, again, this time blotting out some of the detail. I left a faint memory of my true nature: I am not human, I'm a product. *Congratulations, your best friend is a duplicate!*

He fidgeted after a few minutes. Snorted from a short nap and smacked his lips. I was gazing out the window when he opened his eyes. It took a bit for his awareness to catch up to the present moment and the truth of what he was looking at. He was watching me. He considered running. I couldn't blame him. After all that time together, he didn't owe me anything. Maybe he should run.

He leaned forward, then slowly stood, walked next to me. We watched the traffic in the distance, all driving somewhere so unimportant. He propped his leg onto the windowsill and pointed toward the football stadium, leaving a smudge on the glass.

"Remember our first day of school? Jared Miles shoved me down the steps during gym and you pummeled him right there in the bleachers, right in front of the coach and everybody. You remember that?"

"Got suspended three days."

"And he never messed with me again." His eyes darted around. Memories flipped through his mind. "You remember, over there? Remember when Alex Deeter dared me to moon the lacrosse team at practice? You remember that?"

"They came after you with sticks."

"Yeah, and you stood up to all of them."

"They would've beat me senseless if the coach didn't stop them."

"But you took the blame."

"I have a higher pain tolerance."

He tapped the window, punctuating a set of memories as if to validate this moment, to anchor his beliefs about who he was. Who I am. Then he stepped away, scratching his chin. I leaned back against the window, let my head bump against the glass.

Then he said, decisively, "I know who you are, goddamnit."

"I showed you the truth."

"That's not what I mean. I don't care *what* you are. I've known you all my life. You're Socket." He stopped pacing. "Socket Greeny."

He resumed looking out the window. The moments stretched out, silently. The librarians were talking louder, now, mostly about Tommy Fletcher and how he needed to get counseling for his severe attention deficit disorder.

Streeter turned his head. "So what now?"

I shrugged.

"You going to the Garrison?"

"No, it'll just be madness if I go back. I mean, if your alarm system recognized me, I'm not going to make it within a hundred yards before a dozen crawler guards gang-tackle me."

"You can come to my house."

"I... no. Not a good idea."

"Why not? No one will know you're there. Besides, you got to eat."

No, I don't. "It's not that. I'm... evolving into something, I think. I don't think it would be a good idea if you were around me until I figure it out."

"What? You mean, you're becoming one of them?" *He meant duplicate.* "You planning on taking over the human race?"

No, it was the temptation that bothered me. The taste of his essence lingered around me like an addiction. Like a shark smelling blood. I could resist, but for how long?

I faced him. "You feel that in your belly?"

He rubbed his stomach, sensed the fear of falling, the removal of his essence as I let myself for just a moment to reconnect with him, automatically absorbing his essence, leaving him with the twisted missing sensation of a void.

"I think I'm stealing from you," I said. "Kind of like charging my battery with your... life."

He tensed. "Dude, that's cold."

"Sorry."

"Can you stop?"

"Yeah, but... I don't know for how long. I just need to go somewhere with no one around, just for a while, anyway."

The sun hung lower in the sky. Streeter didn't run, but he didn't take his hand away from his stomach, either. His mind was working. After a long minute, he said, "I know where you need to go."

"The North Pole?"

"You need to find your clone."

Now I laughed. Streeter was mentally tough; he assimilated more than I gave him credit for. "I have no idea where he's at."

"I know exactly where he's at." He pulled the locator from his pocket and, fearlessly, took both my hands and placed it in my palms. "Do it again, like you did at the tagghet ceremony. Locate yourself in time and space."

I turned it over, saw my distorted reflection in the black convex surface. It invited me to connect with it, almost like it was thinking to me. *Like we speak the same language.*

"Go on." Streeter nudged me. "Do it."

He had rewritten the code; it was tighter and more efficient, merging with my consciousness as I opened to it. A holographic planet projected from the surface, rotating between us.

"He's there." He stuck his finger on the spot of light in the middle of Illinois. "When you used this at the ceremony, in front of all those people, it knew you were just a copy, it found the original."

A copy. I cringed.

"It worked," he said. "The whole time, it was working."

My chest fluttered. He was right, the locator simply considered me a mirror projected from the original identity. Streeter had done it.

"You should go."

I looked up. "Why?"

"Why? He's you. You're him. You've been separated from who you are all your life. You've got to go see if something will happen."

"Like what?"

"I don't know! What else are you going to do, sit in the desert and meditate the rest of your life? Just go and find out."

Suddenly, I didn't feel in control of anything. And that was my answer. I wasn't in control; I was swept into the current of the unknown, flowing with the mystery of life. I handed the locator back to Streeter. "You're right."

"Hell yeah, I'm right. You can use my car, if you want. I'll tell my gramma you needed it for a couple days. She won't care."

"I won't need it."

"Are you kidding me? Illinois is like 800 miles away unless you've got a ship or something out there in the trees." He looked out the window. "Do you?"

I looked at him. He'd really like to know.

"I'm right, aren't I? Or do you have some kind of teleportation thing." His eyes were wide. "You've got teleportation?"

Maybe I shouldn't do it, I didn't want to overload him again. But he'd want to see it. I held up my hand and let it dissolve. My fingers were the first to fall away, dissolving into the air, followed by my hand, wrist and arm. I gathered the molecules at my waist and my arm reappeared.

"That is badass." He stared at my arm, blinking heavily. The overload was dulling his consciousness again.

"I got to go, Streeter." I washed the thoughts from his immediate awareness, let him keep the memory for later digestion.

"Am I going to see you again?"

"I don't know."

We shook hands, fingers up, then I jerked him close and we hugged, patting each other's backs with the free hand. "You should probably get back to Janette."

"Yeah," he said. "I should, you know." He took a long look, not convinced it wouldn't be the last time he ever saw me, then started away. I'd wait until he was long gone before I leaped. He stopped at the book shelf and turned.

"Thanks, Socket."

"For what?"

"Just, you know. Glad you were here. That's all."

He left before I could say anything. *Glad to be here, Streeter.*

CIVIL WARS

A librarian had come back to make sure no other students were around, but I had dissolved before she turned the corner. I gathered far past Interstate 26, near Monck's Corner and highway 52 and sliced time to a standstill.

I walked the country roads and sometimes went straight through the wetlands. Whenever I felt people within my influence, I turned away. I didn't want to be tempted to draw on their life. I trusted myself less and less, having visions I would leave a wasteland of bodies in my wake. Even the slightest attempt to expand my awareness out like a shrimp net to locate Pike put people into my influence and an immediate download of their essence. Perhaps vampires did exist. We didn't drink blood. Just essence.

Pike was out there, I could sense him, just couldn't locate him. Unlike my original, my *brother;* I had locked onto his location from 800 miles away. He was in Tannerville, Illinois. Population, 12,132. I didn't know his name, but excluding some terrible accident, I assumed he looked like me.

For much of the trip, I saw nothing and heard only the path beneath my feet. I worked my way to the heartland of the Midwest, up through southern Illinois to the central part, where the hills turned flat and the grass was replaced by rows of corn and soybeans. Enormous combine tractors were in the fields in the midst of harvesting another season, a cloud of dust suspended over the long mechanical teeth that would be chopping and stripping the kernels from the cobs once I emerged from the timeslice.

The sun slowly moved higher in the sky, not because time was moving. I walked westerly, from the Eastern Time Zone to Central. A trip in regular time would've taken months, but I arrived on the outskirts of Tannerville at the exact moment I left Charleston. Some twenty miles south of Springfield, I stood on route 29, looking at a sign: *AAAA Girls Basketball State Champions*. I walked near a car travelling sixty miles an hour back in ordinary time; now it was standing still. The license plate read Land of Lincoln.

Abraham Lincoln, the president that freed the slaves.

I grew up in the South where President Lincoln was viewed as a war criminal, by some. Others refused to call it the Civil War. *There was nothing civil about it.* It was the War of Northern Aggression. Even had a history teacher that refused to use the textbook because it was written by Yankees. And here I was, in the Land of Lincoln. My original self, raised in the North. North versus South, the Civil War; a conflict fought long ago, but the scars still remained.

I returned to ordinary time.

I was greeted with the sounds of blackbirds and the distant roar of tractors. Hundreds of feet below, I sensed the coal mine and the men in hardhats and smudged faces, putting in hard hours to pull black rock from the ground. And as they mined the coal, I felt their essence slowly pull towards me, like metal shavings to a magnet. I focused on being centered, but I could only slow the draw. Eventually, I wouldn't even be able to do that.

I couldn't avoid people, now. I walked past small gas stations and Wal-Mart, McDonalds and car dealers, and onto the town square with a clock tower rising from the courthouse. Teenagers hung out by their cars and small business owners hustled inside the clothing stores and jewelry shops. The asphalt road turned to bricks, a town as old as farming.

A couple miles from that, the street ended at a two story white house. It felt like a blank in my consciousness, like it was somehow blocked. Still, I knew he was there.

I stopped at the curb near the mailbox that read *Teck Family*. My stomach fluttered. An old concrete sidewalk led straight to the wide front steps, and at the foot of those steps a girl was doodling with sidewalk chalk. She was singing a song, making up the words as she went. It was a story about a monster that fell in love with a little girl. The monster lived under the bed and he was angry she didn't love him back.

"I don't talk to strangers," she said and went back to drawing with a yellow piece of chalk.

"That's a good idea."

She was humming. I walked gently up the sidewalk and squatted next to her. Her mind was so open and innocent, but I wasn't compelled to draw from her essence, as if the compulsion halted inside a bubble around this house. A warm peacefulness settled in my stomach, relieved I didn't have to focus on restraining myself from taking, that I could just be in this moment.

"What are you drawing?" I asked.

"That's Saucy." She pointed at the girl with big ears and pigtails. "And that's Greg. He's got big teeth." She drew even bigger, sharper teeth on Greg the monster next to Saucy, his mouth open and slobbery.

"He looks mean," I said.

"He can be."

She colored Greg's teeth yellow with big drops of purple stuff dripping off them, humming as she did. She didn't look up, but asked, "Where're you from?"

"Me? I'm from faaaaaar away."

"I'm not four." She frowned at me. "I'm seven years old, you don't have talk to me like a baby."

"Sorry."

She stared at me curiously, then I quickly realized I might look exactly like my original, so I quickly warped my features in her vision, as if she saw my face in a carnival mirror.

"Are you an alien?" she asked.

"What if I am?"

"Then you look pretty normal. For an alien."

"What if I said I wasn't human?"

She shrugged. "Saucy's not human, even though she looks like it. She's my best friend."

Now she was coloring her imaginary friend's hair green. She clapped the dust off her hands and grabbed the thick blue sidewalk chalk and colored Saucy's shoes and started humming again.

"Want to know a secret?" she asked.

"Always."

"Scott got in a fight today."

"Who's Scott?"

"My brother, silly." Her rapid giggle was contagious. "You're here to see him."

"I am?"

"You kind of look like him, you know." She squinted at me with her tongue stuck between her lips. "Well, you do if I do this."

She was giggling again and I couldn't help laughing a little. The essence of joy bubbled between us and it made her laugh harder.

The front door jiggled. "Maddi," her mother called through the screen door. "Time to eat, go wash up."

Maddi smacked her hands again and ran up the wooden steps, past her mother holding the door open. The letter T was in the middle of the screen door. It rattled in the frame as she let it close. "Can I help you?" the mother asked.

"Yes, ma'am. I, uh, was just… uh." I grabbed the railing for support, suddenly dizzy. A powerful force surged from her, gushing inside me. It wasn't her essence. I don't know what it was. And I couldn't read her. I knew nothing about her, not even her name. She could sense the power exchange, and she could sense that I was sensing her sensing me, a loop of self-generating energy, a fusion that was disorienting us both.

"He's here to see Scott, Mama," Maddi said.

Her mother rubbed Maddi's head and whispered for her to go clean up. "Have we met?" the mother asked.

"Um, no—no, ma'am." I stepped lightly up the steps. "I'm kind of new in town, I'm in Scott's class and I, uh, he said I could stop by if I needed help with a project."

Her hair was short, like my mother's, but her hips were wide and her skin sun-baked. She stared intensely and I quickly gathered my focus to distort the perception of my features or she'd be staring at an exact copy of her son. Still, there was nothing I could do about my personal energy she experienced. I felt familiar. Like family.

"There's a school project, ma'am," I said. "Scott's my partner."

"Okay." She opened the door and suddenly smiled. "Well, sure, come in. Come in."

"Thank you."

I stepped inside. A hallway led straight from the front door through an entertainment room to the kitchen in the very back where the aroma of homemade spaghetti filled the house. To the right was a formal living room with light blue walls and expensive, clean furniture. The staircase to the upstairs was on the left, went up next to the wall and then turned right along that wall so that I could see part of the upstairs. Pictures covered the walls below the steps.

Maddi leaned against her mother's leg. "Would you get Scott, dear?" her mother asked.

Maddi watched me on her way to the bottom step, then took a deep breath and shouted, "SCOTT!"

Her mother winced. "Maddi?"

Maddi looked back and rolled her eyes. She walked up the stairs, one step at a time, sliding her hand on the polished railing and watching me as she went.

"If you'll excuse me," the mother said. "Scott will be right down."

Hard music leaked from upstairs when a door opened. Maddi's voice was lost in the beat and a deeper voice responded. They were bickering about something other than the stranger downstairs waiting for him. Maybe Maddi forgot why she went up.

I went to the wall and the wooden floor creaked. The pictures were randomly framed and placed. The last twenty years were captured in photos, starting with a wedding picture, followed by babies and grandparents holding a baby and mother at a baseball game and kids swimming in a pool and someone blowing out candles. The frames were dusty and the glass cracked on a particular one. The picture was somewhat recent.

It was the mother and father standing at the top of the Grand Canyon. The father was holding Maddi when she was only two years old, her hair lighter and curlier, sucking her thumb. The mother had her hands on the shoulders of their son; he was wearing a baseball cap and sunglasses. They were smiling, but not the smile one gives when someone counts to three and they all shout cheese. No, it was like someone said something really, really funny and the smiles came from way down deep.

I touched the glass, dragging a track through the dust, as if I could plug into the joy emanating from a moment captured in time.

The steps thumped like a bowling ball was bouncing down and Maddi went running past, grabbing the post at the bottom and sling-shooting past me toward the kitchen, moaning out the word, "Mooooom."

The music cut off and a door shut upstairs. The steps groaned differently, this time. One at a time. I stepped back toward the door. Scott slid his hand as he took each step deliberately, turning the corner midway and looking at me.

A magnetic force pulled at my stomach. And the closer he got, the stronger it became. It vibrated from my core, chattering in my teeth and under my tongue. The force grew stronger as he reached the bottom step, gushing inside like I was drinking from a fire hydrant. I bumped into the door behind me, grabbed the knob.

It's me.

Every detail. The dour expression. The slight bend in his nose. The relaxed demeanor of his eyes, it was all me. Except for the hair. He had normal brown hair.

He stopped at the bottom step. I held onto the door, afraid I'd be pulled against him. *Is this what it feels like to have the essence sucked out you?*

Shock suddenly opened his eyes a bit wider. He was looking at himself standing in the foyer. I looked down, centered my focus, drew on whatever power I could find to project the illusion of different features. I had to stay focused, or all of them would be looking at Scott's identical twin. When I looked up, the tension eased on his face. He blinked, reset himself, still not sure what was happening. I couldn't tell if he was experiencing what I was feeling. I didn't know anything. I couldn't see his thoughts or motivation or memories. He was completely unknown, and yet his presence was overwhelming me.

"Hey, uh, Scott." I squeezed the doorknob tighter. "You remember… in class, sociology class, we got paired up to do the, uh…" I swallowed. "The project?"

I projected a thought in his direction, hoping it would plant in his mind like a memory, of me sitting behind him in a class that felt like sociology. I couldn't feel his mind, where it began or ended, I could only throw out the suggestion like slinging a dart through the dark, hoping to hit the bull's-eye.

He blinked. "Um…"

"Good, sure. Well, I was wondering if, you know, you had some time to get it out of the way because I've got..." I pointed my thumb behind me, gestured like there were things to do.

He looked down, working hard to recall the project and school, like a dream that begged to be remembered but wasn't really sure if it happened or not. I worked harder at projecting that thought, attempting to make it solid and real. He was getting it, but not believing it.

"Scott, time to eat." His mother stepped between us. Scott stared at her, trying to wake up.

"Scott?" she said. "Are you all right?"

He looked at her, back to me. I was losing him. He was scattered, trying to make sense out of his thoughts and the new ones trying to convince him of a new reality. In one last effort, I threw all my energy into the new reality. *I'm a new student, I sit behind you. We're working on a project. I look nothing like you. I am not you.*

I AM NOT YOU.

He licked his lips, and then clarity settled in. He smiled. "Sure, um, yeah. I'm all right."

His mother smiled, then looked at me. "What's your name?"

"My name is Socket."

"You want to stay for dinner, Socket?"

Scott watched her invite me, then waited for an answer. Like his mother, he was cleared-eyed and settled. They accepted the new reality.

"That's very kind of you," I said.

"Very nice." She started for the kitchen. Scott nodded with a sly smile. I paused at the pictures, gazed once more at the Grand Canyon, recognized the smile looking back.

Like one of the family.

172

A BIG BANG

There were two dogs in the backyard. They'd dug holes near a shed, white paint peeling from the walls, and looked half dead in the shade. I sensed their exhaustion and dreamy thoughts, their legs twitching in a long afternoon nap. Beyond that a pasture was enclosed by an old wooden fence and three horses grazed at the back of the property. Stables were on the other side of the shed and a smaller fenced area with chickens and goats inside.

I was surprised by my level of comfort. My world was standing on its head, but here, inside this house, I didn't feel like an alien. I felt like I was home, like I'd know these people all my life.

Maddi was slopping a spoonful of spaghetti sauce over a mountain of noodles, her eyes big and hungry. Scott was at the table, waiting for the rest of the family. Their mother was near the sink, filling a plastic cup with apple juice.

"What would you like to drink, Socket?" she asked.

"Sweet tea?"

"What's sweet tea?" Maddi asked.

"Um, it's tea with sugar."

"Well, then why don't you just add sugar?"

"I can do that," I said.

Her mother put a tall glass of tea at the table setting next to Scott, along with a bowl of sugar. "Go ahead, Socket, help yourself to some food."

There was no need to eat. I had no appetite. But I got myself a small helping, savoring the scent of homemade sauce. It wasn't so much the spices and tomato sauce that I savored, but the effort that went into making it. The entire house had a special energy, one that was lived-in, the intermingling of a family essence that wove tightly through the walls.

They were waiting for me to sit. Maddi already had noodles spun on her fork. As soon as my butt hit the chair, they were in her mouth. The meal began. There was another setting at the head of the table, like someone else was coming but not until later.

Things were spinning, like I was the one in an alternate reality, eating next to my identical twin. It could be easy to forget I didn't belong. Easy to believe I didn't really exist, but I let myself believe it. For the moment, I belonged.

There was nothing but the sound of knives on plates and spinning forks. Scott ate without issue. Maddi was moaning with each bite, eyeballing me. I slowly cut the noodles and pushed the food around. I wasn't fooling her, so I took a bite.

"You know, it's kind of weird that Scott's friend is eating with us," Maddi said. "I mean, we just met him."

"Mind your manners, dear," the mother said.

"I'm just *saaaaaying*…" she sang.

The mother stopped chewing and glared. Maddi slurped a noodle into her mouth like a worm running for cover. I smiled at her and she laughed, splashing sauce all over her lips.

"Where are you from, Socket?" the mother asked.

"South Carolina."

"I thought you sounded a bit Southern."

"Yes, ma'am."

"Is Socket a southern name?" Maddi asked.

174

"I don't believe so."

"Well, if you were born there, why don't you have a Southern name?"

Because I wasn't born. I shrugged.

"You know what your name sounds like?" Maddi said. "Like Scott's name."

Her mother stopped chewing and thought about it. "Oh, yes, you're right, Maddi. It does sound like it."

I frowned, thinking also, but coming up blank. "Ma'am?"

"Scott Teck," she said. "Sock-et."

And there you go. Mystery solved over a plate of spaghetti. My name was an aberration of my original, a scrambling of sounds and letters. Perhaps I wasn't a weapon after all. Just a reflection.

"Isn't that odd, Scott?" the mother said.

He looked at me, taking another bite, nodding. I looked away, but not too quickly. I couldn't look into his eyes, it started the magnetic pull in my stomach, and each time it got stronger. I was able to resist, as long as I wasn't looking at him. Fortunately, he was more interested in eating.

"What's your middle name?" the mother asked.

"Pablo."

"Oh, my gosh!" Maddi clapped and pointed at Scott. "Tell him your middle name, Scott. Tell him! Tell him!"

He hovered over his plate, noodles dangling, shaking his head.

"Scott doesn't like his middle name," the mother said.

"Can I tell him, Mama?" Maddi asked, bouncing. "Can I? Can I?"

"Picasso," Scott said. "My middle name is Picasso, isn't that awesome?"

Maddi slumped in her chair, about as much as I did. Pablo Picasso, one of humanity's most celebrated artists, a well-spring of creativity, the essence of being human. Would Pablo be whole without Picasso? Could something be creative if it was separated at birth?

And the hits just keep on coming.

"What's your project about?" the mother asked.

"Ma'am?"

"The school project?"

There was a moment when the family looked at each other, a moment where the new reality faltered and a stranger was sitting at the table. I got out of my thoughts and focused. "Project, oh, yeah," I said. "It's a sociology project. We're supposed to, uh, interview each other about family. You know, your parents and grandparents, where you were born, that sort of thing."

"That sounds interesting," she said. "You didn't tell me about this project, Scotty."

He shrugged, mouth full.

"We're *adooopted*." Maddi hunched over her plate with a devious smile, not asking for permission to give the answer this time. Her mother told her to pay attention to dinner and Maddi looked at me from the corners of her eyes, her feet thumping on her chair.

The back door in the pantry closed and the father marched into the kitchen. "Sorry, guys. My meeting ran late." He hung his keys on a rack next to the doorframe and went directly to the stove. While he shoveled food onto his plate, he looked out the window over the sink. "Mary Ellen? Did someone let the chickens out?"

"Oh, the gate must not have got closed," the mother said. "Maddi, can you get them?"

"I got to do everything." She dropped her fork on the plate.

"That's because you're Cinderella, honey." She whacked her on the fanny as she went out the back door. "How was the meeting, Joey?"

"You know meetings." The father sat down and started eating, saying with food in his mouth, "Who's our guest?"

The mother looked at Scott. He wiped his mouth. "Oh, he's a friend from school. Stopped by to work on a… project, I think. Um, his name is Socket."

176

Joey's arms were tan and hairy. The fatherly essence was rich and powerful. The energy in the room changed with his presence. It was stronger and tighter, enveloped the whole house. With him at the table, the family was complete. I was whole and unbroken.

"Have I met you?" he asked.

"No, sir."

"So, what kind of name is Socket?"

Maddi and the mother told him about my name and how it sounded like Scott Teck, and the father nodded and listened and laughed. Maddi told their father about the South and how they were learning about the Civil War at school and Scott got up to get more food. Fortunately, no one paid attention that my plate had hardly been touched, how I expertly scattered the food like I'd eaten as much as I could. Instead, I sat back and experienced the flow. The conversation soon turned to Maddi's classmate that threw up at recess and Scott's ex-girlfriend working at the grocery store and their mother's appointment at the church. The sorts of things families talk about at dinner, I suppose.

And I was there, right in the middle of it all.

Maddi had cleared off the table and piled the dishes in the sink, then went into the backyard with her parents. Scott filled the sink with soapy water and stacked the dishes on the counter.

"Dishwasher broke?" I asked.

"You're looking at the dishwasher." He threw a dishtowel over his shoulder.

"I'll wash, if you dry," I said.

"Deal." He shifted to the left side of the sink. I stepped in his place and sunk my hands into the warm soapy water, grabbed a plate and rubbed it clean with a soft sponge. Scott rinsed and dried and put it in the cabinet.

It was getting near dark outside. Our reflections were clear in the window that looked into the side yard. Mary Ellen and Joey were sitting in fray lawn chairs watching Maddi throw a slimy ball to the dogs. Scott hardly looked up, focused on the dishes coming his way. We were in sync, a washing tandem. Identical twins, the difference only in the color of hair. *Why the white hair? Was it an error in the cloning, or a hint at my transparency?*

How many times had I washed dishes, all alone, not knowing *I* was washing dishes somewhere else in the world? And now we were linked, our energy coupled like trains. His strength was growing, absorbing my own like I was doing to others, yet I couldn't tell if he could feel it. He didn't appear to be aware of anything other than the dishes and warm water, yet I experienced him as a massive star whose gravitational pull locked onto me, unable to free myself. It was only a matter of time before I was swallowed. I wasn't sad about that. Wasn't anything. It seemed that's the way things were supposed to be.

Maddi's laughter drifted through the window and the dogs barked. And I washed another bowl. Scott rinsed. For once, I wasn't saving the world. Maybe it was saving me.

Scott went to his room, upstairs to the left. *This is Scott's Room* was on the door. The walls were covered with pictures, mostly hard-edge bands in concert. He was at the desk, flipping the pages on a skateboard magazine with the likes of Josiah Gatlyn grinding a handrail and Benny Fairfax nailing something impossible.

"I can't wait until I'm done with school," he said.

"Where you going?"

"Anywhere but here." He turned the page.

It was completely dark outside. The lawn chairs were empty. It took everything I had to stand three feet away from Scott. The draw was undeniable. I was leaning away from him.

But it was no longer to be denied.

"I got to go," I said.

"What about the project?"

I turned, looked into his face. *My* face. *My* eyes. "It's just about done."

I stopped resisting, let go of the energy bundled in my stomach. It flowed like Hoover dam had tumbled. The influx hit him in the gut. He convulsed like he was about to puke. His skin was quaking. He was draining me.

"What's... what's happening?" He couldn't get up, couldn't get away. He had to sit, to claim what was rightfully his. I was only his shadow, his reflection, and I had so much to give.

As the darkness crept over me, I extended my hand to shake. "Take it," I said.

His head was shaking.

But he wasn't looking at my hand, he was seeing my face. I could not pretend anymore. He saw my true nature, saw his own face looking back. Even if I wasn't real, if I was just a reflection, I was grateful to have had the opportunity to exist. To feel. To love. I didn't know what would happen when it was over, where I would go or what I would become. There was only this moment. And it had reached an end.

"Go on," I said. "It's all right."

Reality was breaking up, his mind began to quiver. But he held onto consciousness, not able to comprehend the impossible moment that appeared out of an ordinary day, his own self standing in his bedroom, reaching out.

His hand moved slowly. Darkness was taking my vision as it moved toward my open palm, as if I was dissolving from the physical world. As if I was returning to the great void of the moment. I did not see him take my hand. I did not feel his sweaty palm grip mine.

But I knew when it did.

It was an explosion.

My mind expanded like the Big Bang, scattered in all directions, through all the elements in a painless flight.

I did not see. Did not smell. But I was aware. Felt my life drain away from my body, through my hand and into Scott. He absorbed what was rightfully his. He was the original face. My memories would be his. My life was his.

He would remember my father holding his hand at the fair, how he ate dinner with my mother, watched them bury my father, and the endless fights in South Carolina. How he fell in love with

Chute. Every moment filled him, became his memories. It was his life, now.

And when I was empty, his memories began to leak into my awareness. I saw Scott's life, from the very beginning. I experienced memories, both conscious and subconscious, of his life from the very first breath he took. Felt his body slide from my mother's womb, the expansion of his chest and the blurry face of my mother hovered over him, her fulfilling nipple in his mouth and the warm embrace of my father.

And I felt the cold fate of his reality.

He was swept away, cuddled in a warm blanket that was no substitute for the woman who gave birth to him. He was too young to know that a blind man had plans for him, for all of us. Pivot took him far away where he was adopted by a warm and loving family.

His life was not much different than mine, the struggles were similar, the details different. He was introverted and righteous, carried a deep yearning to know the meaning of his life, always sensing something greater was out there, but found himself stuck in life's mundane moments.

He got very ill during a swine flu epidemic.

Fell out of a tree and broke his arm when he was ten.

Caught a twelve pound bass in Tannerville Lake.

Hiked Pike's Peak in Colorado on a family vacation, had his own dirt bike, carried his sister home when she was hit with a rock, one he threw, her face covered with blood, the scar still above her left eye, won an art contest in third grade, stole a book from school, changed his grades, kissed a girl behind the garage...

His life settled in my awareness like a new body of water. Deep and clear. Still.

The darkness was calm.

And I remained. I was still there. I was still me, still intact.

Complete.

And my consciousness gathered back in Scott's room. Perhaps I disappeared during the experience. Or maybe I was there the entire time, experiencing it on another level. But when I returned, my feet were on the carpet and my hands at my side. Scott was on the floor. His eyes rolled back and twitching.

I picked him up, lay him on his bed. Even in the solitude of unconsciousness, his mind was coping with the reality of his new memories, the awareness of his true birthright. He was only human.

You are more than human, Pivot told me. *No human could do what you have done, and yet I needed a human to do it.*

I sat next to Scott. He was no longer a mystery, his mind completely available to me, for he was no longer separate. I moved my awareness inside his mind and soothed the conflict rumbling through his being, sorting through the new memories trying to find a place to be accepted. I gathered all those memories that he received from me and hid them in the darkness of his subconscious. One day, he would know them, when he was ready to see the truth, they would emerge, slowly. One at a time. But for now, he needed to just be Scott.

Thank you, I said to him. To me. Sleeping peacefully in his bed.

I peeked into Maddi's room where she was sound asleep, squeezing a doll against her cheek with her thumb in her mouth, her tongue clicking.

I snuck downstairs where their father was watching Sportscenter and mother was reading a magazine. They didn't hear the floorboards creaking as I stood unnoticed in the doorway, taking one last moment to experience the family essence centered in the room. I slipped outside, still unnoticed.

In the middle of the brick street, under the buzzing street light, I stood on a manhole cover. The stars filled the sky and night fell quietly on the small town of Tannerville. I took a deep breath, filling my lungs with the breath of the entire world, feeling its struggles, its pain and happiness, loss and gain, birth and death. The human essence contained the beauty of life, the essence of which contained darkness and light, the pure joy of

181

life, hidden only by a lack of understanding. But it was there, not to be gotten, not something that was missing. Only something that needed to be seen.

And somewhere in the world, I felt every consciousness struggle with its own existence, each soul rightfully searching for itself. And among them, I sensed the awareness of Pivot, like he was everywhere, as if he had yet to gather his body in a particular place in space and time.

There was another presence out there. This being was intimately familiar, shining like a beacon, calling me to join him. He was in Charleston. And he was waiting for me to arrive. It was a bald man that walked freely down a sidewalk.

GAME CHANGER

Downtown Charleston.

Tourists crowded the sidewalk, holding hands and walking casually past art studios, pausing in front of picture windows. They lined up outside Hymen's Seafood for a late bite or crowded at Comiskey's for desert. Just another night.

I was in front of the long market, the building painted mustard yellow and Charleston green. Pike was somewhere in the crowd, his presence scattered like a game of Hide-and-Seek.

A street vendor sawed away on a beat up fiddle, curled up against the wall with a box of coins in front of him. Tourists occasionally stopped to toss in a bill, and the guy nodded curtly. I walked past him, looked down the street left of the market, recalled the vision of when Pike walked free, trying to remember what side of the market he was on. But there were no details in the vision. Just the street. And the girl.

I closed my eyes and leaned against the building. He has been here already, I could feel him, but what was he waiting for? In the vision, it was dark and the streets were crowded with slow moving traffic. A rickshaw bicycle rang a bell. And there was no fiddle playing, either.

"You want a rose?" A kid held out a palm leaf torn and folded to look like a beige rose. "Ten dollars for one, twenty for two."

"No, thanks," I said.

"All right, how about five dollars for one?"

The music had stopped. The musician's box was still on the sidewalk, filled with coins and his violin. A note was tucked between the strings. *Looking for me?*

Pike's presence was smeared on the paper like a fingerprint. He was disguising himself as the fiddle player, but how? I looked around and then closed my eyes, reaching out with my mind, feeling each individual presence mingle throughout the market. I felt their movements, their desires and fears, but none were Pike.

A stick poked between my fingers. I looked at the palm rose in my hand. The boy was twirling one. "You want to buy another?"

"I didn't buy this one."

"That guy over there bought it for you, said you looked lost, like you needed a friend. Said you'd buy another."

"Where?"

"Buy another and I tell you." He held the rose up to my face. "Ten bucks."

I knelt in front of him, gently took his shoulders. I knew his life, and it had been hard. But I couldn't change him, couldn't tap him with a magic wand to make it better. At the moment, I just needed to see what the man looked like and where he went. I scanned his recent memory and saw the man was bald with dark glasses, smiling at the kid like he was looking at someone else, like he knew I'd see the memory. *You're so close.*

I looked to the left side of the market again. There, along the sidewalk, people were hustling out of the way. I ran across the street, around traffic, between the parked rickshaws. Up ahead, the bald man. *Pike.* He scattered the crowd like a bad smell. And then my vision materialized.

The family and the little girl, pulling her gum out of her mouth, her mother chastising her for it, reaching down to yank her hand back, not seeing the little man whose force slammed into them. The father was thrown against a parking meter and his wife back into him, but the little girl's hand slipped from her grip. She tumbled into the road, in front of a car that was going too fast.

I cut into time, freezing it the instant the bumper reached her forehead, inches from splitting it open. I walked through the silent night and removed her from danger, lay her at her mother's feet.

Pike's gone, again.

I returned to normal time. The tires screeched. The mother screamed. A crowd gathered around the frightened girl, crying on her mother's shoulder. I stood beneath the awning of the storefront where the owners rushed out to ask if anyone was hurt, they had already called the police. But the assailant was gone.

Suddenly, I caught a whiff of his presence, floating on the wind. Across the street, he'd entered the long market, slipping beneath a canvas curtain. Traffic stopped. A cop had already arrived on foot, taking a description of the strange, bald man. I walked unnoticed between the cars, pulled the canvas aside and stepped inside.

During the day, it was crowded with vendors and tourists, but at night it was empty and lonely aside from a bird searching for a place to nest. The city sounds were muffled by the canvas walls. At the far end, near the side road that crossed between the buildings, a short man was hunkered over a fat woman and a display of sweetgrass baskets.

[Please, leave.] I planted the thought in the woman's mind.

She looked at me across the great distance. Months of hard work lay on the ground in front of her, and I was suggesting she leave them behind. Pike slowly turned his head, his black glasses like holes on his face.

"Do you mind?" he said. "WE'RE HAGGLING!"

The basket woman placed her bundle of grass on the ground and got up, dusting off her dress, and walked away.

"Great," Pike said. "That's just great. Do you know how hard it is to find a quality sweetgrass basket these days?" He shook a dark banded basket at me. "They weave these motherfuckers by hand and charge a ton of money. And she was going to give it to me for free. For free, you understand?"

He was a projection, that's why I couldn't locate him. There were no projectors around, so I didn't know how he was doing it, I just knew I couldn't locate him. I attempted to penetrate his image, follow it back to the source, but it was empty. Pike dropped the basket and spread his arms, as if to help.

"It's like magic, isn't it?" he said. "In case you're wondering, and I know you are, I'm taking advantage of the plethora, that's right I said plethora, of virtualmode portals in the downtown area. I'm using them to project this wonderful image in front of you." He spread his arms, again. "It's a little trick you might learn one of these days, if you're lucky."

"Is this a game to you?"

"It's all a game, wouldn't you say?" He dropped his arms. "I mean, everything is useless, just a game for the gods And where does it end, huh? Where does it all end, wonderboy? Because now you know the truth, don't you. You know who we're doing our little song and dance for." He pointed up.

He's known all along. He knew I wasn't human. He knew Fetter was out there. Why hadn't I seen it before?

"Look at you," he said, clasping his hands over his heart, "all grown up and realized. You're a big boy now, your master must be proud. Is he? Is Papa Pivot happy that his boy is all grown up and out there saving the world?" He swung a left and right hook through the air. "You're out there fighting the good fight, looking for the bad people, eh?"

"He's not my master."

"Oh, but isn't he divine and wonderful? All pure of heart, like an angel sent from heaven to save the human race, wouldn't you say?"

"How did you know?"

"How did I know?" His piercing laughter bounced around the enclosed market. "How did I... oh, that's rich, wonderboy. How did I know? I knew from the second I saw you." The canvas walls fluttered. "I saw through you that very first day you came to the Garrison, wonderboy. All doe-eyed and goody, I smelled Pivot on you like a seven day corpse."

"You've known all this time?"

"Who do you think I am? Seriously, for being wonderboy, you're not that bright—"

"You need to exit the market." A man stepped into view. "No one's allowed... "

Pike turned on the man, his anger impacting him like a wave of atomic heat. It was only the embrace of my mind around him that kept Pike's wrath from stripping his mind clean, but it still knocked him backwards and out of sight.

"You can't save them all," Pike said. "Besides, what's the point? They're all heading for the great black planet in heaven anyway. You only delay the inevitable."

"How could you know about all this? How could you elude the minders and the Paladins?"

"Everyone knows! Every one of these skinbags, these buckets of worm food, know their life is futile, a waste of effort! They all know, wonderboy, right here, they feel it." He thumped his chest. "They know there's something wrong with their existence, that their gods are just playing them. They just refuse to face the fact that they're rats in the wheel."

"That's why you hate being human, is that it? You want to be absorbed by Fetter, just to get it over with."

"You still don't get it? You don't see?" He yanked off his glasses and marched closer, white eyes blazing in the dim light. "Let me know when you do."

I still couldn't feel him. *Couldn't feel him*. He had a presence, but no sensation of essence. But that could only mean... "You've already converted."

"Oh, you're getting warmer."

"You're a duplicate."

"You're red-hot!"

There has always been a mystery about Pike. They wouldn't kill him. He endured torture beyond what was humanly possible. He was never meant to survive, but he did. He always survived. Because...

"You've always been a duplicate."

"WE GOT A WINNER!" He whooped and hollered and leaped and danced, swinging his arms over his head in wild celebration.

Outside, the sirens rang out and voices crowded around the market. A few people peeked around the corner. A policeman walked inside with the father of the little girl. He nodded at Pike who was now doing something of a foxtrot.

"Can I speak to you a moment, sir?" the policeman asked.

Pike stopped mid-step. He put on his black glasses and wiggled his eyebrows. He pursed his lips as the policeman slowed his approach, putting his hand on his sidearm, sensing danger.

"Sir, I need you to put your hands where I can see them!"

Pike drew a whistling breath between his lips. The temperature in the market suddenly dropped.

"I need you to—"

His face paled. And Pike drew deeper. The policeman dropped to his knees. Pike was drawing out the man's essence, absorbing it like a parasite. Then the crowd began shouting outside as he drew on them, too. People were falling, screaming. I felt them weaken and clutch their stomachs as they felt the essence of their lives siphoned away.

I stiffened, throwing out my awareness like a protective bubble, penetrating every person within a square mile, coating their consciousness like a membrane. Pike smacked his lips.

"It's like a cool, minty rush, isn't it?" He flicked his tongue under his cheeks and lips. "Tingles the tongue. You need to get some of that, wonderboy. There's only so much to go around."

He knelt next to the policeman, struggling to breathe. "Would you be so kind as to leave us alone?" Pike asked. "We're having a private conversation. Thank you."

The policeman crawled away, pushing the canvas wall open and gasping for air.

"And tell your friends," Pike called through his hands. "We'll be done soon."

It was all I could do to contain Pike's influence. While I felt limitless in the desert, I felt more human since merging with Scott. Maybe since I wasn't stealing life, I was running out of it.

"Look at you." Pike walked near me, pretended to wipe a bead of sweat off my cheek. "You try so hard to save them. And for what?"

"They're real."

"Is that right?"

More sirens sang. Police were listening to the stories of what was going on. It wouldn't be long before they stormed inside.

"It stung when you discovered the truth, didn't it," he said, sharply. "When you found out what you really are, it hurt. Am I right? One day, you're walking around, doing good, helping people, saving the world, making a difference, paving a path to heaven then *thhhhhhppt,* you find out you're just a pawn." He pinched his fingers together. "Stings, just a bit."

"No more than watching you murder."

"They're already dead. They just don't know it."

"They're the reason I'm here."

"You're... you? You're here because of... oh, I get it." He wagged his finger over his head. "Yes, yes! Pivot created you to save them! Well, isn't that just grand and holy of him. Isn't that just divine, that he only thinks of them. Wouldn't you say, because he certainly doesn't care about you or any other pawn in his game." He ground his teeth. "We're all just pawns. The question is, do you want to keep playing?"

"You don't have to do this."

"Open your eyes, wonderboy! You're doing exactly what he wants you to do. It's all part of his plan, his great master plan to save the universe from the evil of humankind's very own creation."

"Fetter still exists."

"I know, I know." He waved me off. "You're the savior that brought her back, blah, blah, blah… Why do you think I let you live, huh?"

"*YOU, IN THE MARKET.*" A policeman's voice crackled over a speaker. "*YOU NEED TO COME OUT WITH YOUR HANDS BEHIND YOUR HEAD. I REPEAT, COME OUT—*"

Pike threw his hands out to the sides. A sub-sonic wave thumped through the ground, shaking the walls. Despite my efforts, many people fell unconscious. The police abruptly reorganized to evacuate the area, calling for reinforcements.

"So fucking annoying!" Pike shook his head. "Anyway, where was I?"

He hurt them. How was he doing this? Even if he was here, in the flesh, the display of power was beyond me. But he was doing it through a projection! I felt my body shrink as I continued to protect the innocent.

"Did he tell you that you're special, is that it?" Pike said. "Is that why you're so dedicated to them, mmm? Is it because you met your original self, got to merge with your soul, is that why you're so irrational? Let me guess." He looked very serious, spoke in a gritty tone. "*Socket, you're the only one that can help them. You are the one. The One. Just like in The Matrix. That's you.*"

Pike tilted his head, like he was studying something genuinely curious.

"Do you know what happened to my original?" He put his finger in his mouth and cocked his thumb, jerked his head back. "Blew his goddamn head off his shoulders."

"Original?"

"Oh, you didn't know? Where are my manners?" He slapped his thigh, then extended his hands in consolation. "Pivot made me, too. Did I forget to tell you? Yeah, I was his first attempt to fool the Almighty Fetter." He spoke into the back of his hand, like he was telling a secret. "So you see, you're not that special after all."

"Impossible."

"The hits just keep coming, don't they?"

"He wouldn't have let you live."

"He can't kill me, wonderboy. He created a monster, yes indeed. And in case you haven't noticed, they can't kill you, either. But nothing will get in the way of the Papa Pivot's master plan, bring forth the devil," – he took a short bow, then gestured to me – "or the savior."

As long I live, so will he.

"Listen, there's not much time left before these morons march in here with their weapons and begin shooting air, so let me make you an offer before I have to vaporize their asses into cockroach shit." Pike bounced his fingertips together gleefully. "I feel sorry for you, wonderboy. Really, I do. You're young and naïve. You still have emotions and feel for these lab rats. It's all very confusing, I know. It's tough to be a teenager these days, really it is. But it's time to grow up."

"Pike—"

"Just listen." He held up a finger. "Pivot is a master, I'm not denying that. After all, he's going after the greatest predator that has ever existed. He wants to take down Fetter, something that has survived for billions and billions of years, in measurable time. In order to take down a tiger that size, he's had to sacrifice a few lambs along the way. So how do you capture a jewel thief? You dangle the shiniest diamond right in her face." He gestured to me. "You, wonderboy, you are the jewel. Fetter couldn't resist. So do you think he needs you any more? Pivot still believes he's god, am I right?"

"Why didn't you just tell me this earlier, huh? Why all the games and clues and deception?"

"Now what fun would that be? Besides, I needed you to bring Fetter back." He jabbed at the ground like a lawyer making his final argument. "The game is about to change."

"I already delivered Fetter to Pivot."

Pike looked around, feeling the reinforcements arrive outside. Blue lights flashed beneath the canvas walls. Hundreds of boots scuffed the pavement. It would take everything I had to protect them.

"I'm going to relieve Pivot of his duty," he said.

"I can't help you. I won't."

"Loyal to Pivot?"

"I will destroy you."

"I'm counting on it." Pike sneered. "And in return, I'll find a special place for you in the universe. You can be my first in command, once you stop all this nonsense. After all, we're brothers, you and me. All part of Pivot's big happy family."

"You're no better than Fetter."

"I am what I am."

"You're nothing."

"As are you."

As I released my mind from protecting the people outside, I felt a thread of his presence slip through the veil that hid his true location. It was faint and delicate, but I could follow it, I just needed time. I couldn't let him destroy them. Not the human race. He was right, I had no reason, but I loved them, even if it was just emotion for my mother, for Streeter. For Chute.

"IT'S NOT RIGHT!" I shouted.

"It's the law! Evolution! Man was made in the image of God and I was made in the image of man, therefore, I will become god. I will become a god, an unforgiving one. I will strike these motherfuckers with reckless abandon and devour what is mine. I will become the black planet that absorbs the universe, all that is, until all is gone. The universe will beg for forgiveness. And I will remind them... some sins cannot be forgiven."

"I won't let you."

"Then stop me."

He smiled and opened his presence. I pressed forward, shooting my awareness through it, following his projection with my mind, slithering through space and time, across the world, into the mountains, into the ground, slamming into Pike's skin.

He stood unrelenting on a stone slab, knowing I was watching, I was seeing. Behind him, the grimmet tree.

The Garrison!

I returned to my body. "I'll be right there."

"Don't dally."

"YOU HAVE THIRTY SECONDS TO COME OUT WITH YOUR HANDS BEHIND YOUR HEAD!"

"And one more thing," Pike said.

"WE WILL FIRE. I REPEAT, WE WILL FIRE."

Canisters of tear gas shot beneath the tarps and rattled over the floor, releasing noxious clouds.

"TEN SECONDS."

Pike pursed his lips. Drew a deep breath.

"FIVE, FOUR..."

Before I could reach out to protect the thousands of innocent minds, darkness settled over downtown like a blanket. The canvas walls shredded. Cars flipped and bodies tumbled through the streets. Windows shattered. Screams.

There was a bright light. I didn't hear the explosion, but I felt the ground lurch. I was spinning above the market. I felt the city cry. I felt their panic in my chest. And before I landed somewhere far away, I heard Pike's final thought.

[God will be dead.]

REFUEL

She was old. Maybe seventy. I didn't know her name or her exact age. I could barely open my eyes. Her brown wrinkled face was soft. She smelled like roses.

"Just relax, honey," she spoke, quietly. "Help is on the way."

I was on the wide concrete steps leading up to the Customs House, almost two blocks from the market. My body was twisted at an odd angle. As my senses returned, the smell of smoke and crushed concrete overshadowed the woman's scent. The streetlights were dead, but the dark sky flickered orange from fire somewhere in the market. I looked around but the woman put her hand on my forehead, shooshing me to relax.

"Nowhere to go, right now, honey."

The perfume on her wrist was strong. She patted my cheek, making sure the only thing I could see was her face. Her eyes involuntarily flicked down to something she didn't want me to see. Gravel and debris were scattered on the steps, along with charred boards and metal.

Sirens were interspersed with cries for help and military orders. Blue and red lights ran across the walls and the old woman patted my face, singing a hymnal song without the words, humming lovely tones in her throat. Pain began to vibrate along my back and I was finally able to take a physical inventory of my condition. My pelvis was shattered and there were deep contusions along my ribs and liver and kidney. If that wasn't enough, my left lung was completely deflated. I tried to move but felt nailed to the steps. A rusty iron rod was driven through my back and poked out between my ribs.

My strength was returning quickly, but I wasn't sure how. I brought my nervous system under control, quelling the sensations of pain. I was stronger, but still not enough to see with my mind, so I looked left and right, the streets filled with ambulances and fire trucks. EMTs ran with orange boxes. How long had I been on the steps?

"Help is coming," she said, mistaking my eye movement as panic. "Don't you worry."

A surge of strength emanated from her, filling my body, quickly healing broken bones. I shifted my legs to reconnect my pelvis, moving just enough to straighten out, even as she tried to keep me still. I reattached crucial arteries and repaired damaged organs. All that was left was the metal rod.

A pair of emergency workers in white shirts jogged past with keys jangling.

"Excuse me, excuse me!" the woman shouted. "This boy needs some help, please."

"We'll be right there, ma'am," one shouted back.

"Okay, okay," she said, putting her hands back on my face and starting her song again. "They'll be right here, honey."

"Please, no," I said, spitting out the words with only one working lung. "Others… need help."

"Shoo-shoo-shoooo." She touched my lips. "No talking, help is coming."

I could feel her mind, now. Her name was Anna. She was seventy-four years old. She'd lived downtown all her life. She had four children and twelve grandchildren. She went to church on Sundays and rarely uttered a bad word. And she called most people honey. And it was her strength that was filling. Not so much her strength, but her love and genuine caring for me, lying on the steps of the Custom's House with a fatal wound bubbling from my chest. She stopped to help me die, if she was honest. She stopped so the last thing I would see was a caring face. So I would not die alone.

I wouldn't have died without her, but I would've lain helpless unless I stole essence from those around me to recover. Right now, they needed all the strength they could get.

"Okay, ma'am." An EMT took a knee next to me, opening his box near my head. "Let me take a—" He choked after spotting the metal rod, even jerked back. He looked at the other EMT on the other side, both knowing their only recourse was to make me comfortable in my last few minutes.

Anna sat near my head. She took my hand and patted it while her song trickled between our palms. My awareness began to expand outward, penetrating the EMTs and the pedestrians standing back. They all held the same thoughts: *Terrorism.* Somebody blew the downtown up, but for what? Religion? Politics? Or had the duplicates finally returned?

AI is back, baby.

Some of the pedestrians were filming us and my fatal wound would be uploaded to the Internet. "How's that dude still alive?"

Stella, the female EMT, prepared a sedative patch to administer to my neck while Jake, the other EMT, took my wrist. He moved his fingers around then pressed on my neck. "He doesn't have a pulse."

"Well, he's alive," Stella said.

"Yeah, I got that, but I can't find his pulse."

Stella tried and failed, too, then figured it was too weak to find and slapped the sedative patches on my neck anyway. They were wasting their time, other people needed help. But they gave their time selflessly. Their concern for others, like Anna, seeped inside me. In fact, the more I expanded, the more I felt the selfless acts of courage. Of firemen rushing into burning buildings. Emergency workers risking their lives. Of the police, protecting the innocent. The courageous acts of love beamed from them like an excess fountain of essence, filling the atmosphere, searching for a place to give. And it filled me until I had the strength to influence the people around me, the ones attempting to save me, a dying boy that didn't stand a chance.

[Thank you,] I thought to them. *[Please go, help others.]*

It took a moment for the thought to register, and then the EMTs loaded their boxes, answered a call and rushed toward the market to help a SWAT member injured in the explosion. The pedestrians watched them leave, then turned the recorder off, wandered away, out of the area. All that was left was Anna, humming with her eyes closed, shaking her head as she did. Hoping for a miracle.

My hands were charred black from the explosion. I sat up, felt the ribbed metal rod pull from my chest, things popping as it slurped out the back. It took a few moments to repair my lung and close the wound. My shoes were missing, having been blown off, charring my feet as black as my hands.

I took her hand and soothed her thoughts, convinced her that she had saved a dying boy simply by stopping and being present with him. In fact, she might've saved the world.

I removed the memory of my fatal condition, left no trace of the broken body she found impaled on the steps.

"Thank you, Anna."

She opened her eyes. "You're welcome, honey."

And when she was ready, I helped her stand and guided her down the steps, watched her walk away from the market, watched until she turned the corner and was safely out of sight.

There was so much to do in the market, but I was needed elsewhere, a place where the entire world needed me. If Pike wasn't stopped, there could be war zones like this everywhere. I didn't have the strength to dissolve and gather across space-time, could not waste it on slicing time. But there was still a way to get there.

I pulled a motorcycle from the rubble and touched the ignition, feeling the engine whir into life. Quietly, I raced from the scene, speeding between traffic, the sirens drifting off behind me. I plunged into a darkened city, a helpless city, a reeling human race. I headed for a wormhole that would take me to the Garrison.

THE FACELESS ONE

Across the field, the tall cold wall of Garrison Mountain appeared. It was daylight, but the sky was cast with gray clouds, casting pale light across a shadowless field. A cool breeze scoured my cheeks, watering my eyes. The mountain grew as I sped down the path winding through the boulders, looming with the gray sky over its shoulder, bearing down on me. I locked the back tire, sliding to a stop at the base of the mountain. I took a moment to expand my awareness, to sense what was inside. I was breathing hard, anxiety constricting my muscles.

I hardly had the range, the energy, to feel what was inside. The air carried tones of stillness and caution, but inside was a mystery. There was no more waiting. I stepped through the wall and its cold illusion, and into the dank garage.

Silence.

Danger pricked my awareness.

Several rotund servys, the size of exercise balls, lay still in the center, leaning against each other. No eyelights glowing. No movement as I approached. They had been deactivated. And beyond, near the leaper, was the body of a Paladin. Dressed in formal uniform, he was on his back, as if he'd just fallen asleep. There was no blood mixed with his red hair, but a sizeable knot where he hit the floor. His skin was cold.

Tingles the tongue.

I touched his neck, his chest and forehead, searching for traces of memory that might tell me what happened, but his entire life had been absorbed. No human would withstand the loss of essence. Paladins, even the most highly trained, wouldn't stand a chance against Pike. All this time, he had been biding his time, enduring years of suffering, playing possum, until now. And all this time, he had been held captive in the catacombs of the Garrison, deep below ground. Pike had everything he needed, he was just waiting. *For what?*

I shut the Paladin's eyelids.

He must've been entering the garage from the leaper, had to be caught by surprise, his weapon still firmly attached to his belt, his hand not even near it. I approached the leaper, commanded a destination with a thought but it did not respond, as lifeless as the servys. I penetrated its circuitry, reactivated its processor, and the walls were glowing again. I repeated my destination. I had a feeling Pike would not be hard to find.

I would start with the Preserve.

If Chute was here, the rest of the world would have to wait.

Something was wrong.

I knew it before the leaper arrived at the entrance, before I stepped into the Preserve. Something beyond what I saw in the garage, on a much more massive scale. I couldn't feel the Preserve vibrate inside me, the raw energy of a thousand species of animals and insects. Even before I stepped through the leaper wall, I sensed the silence.

The soundlessness of death.

While the leaves were green and the scent of the forest was rich and earthy, not a single bird, mammal or insect scratched the trees, sang out or barked. The air hung thick and motionless.

I ran for the tagghet field, through shortcuts of undergrowth. And the deeper I got into the jungle, the heavier it felt. The quieter it became. Only the sounds of my breathing and quickened steps as I jerked vines away. The images of Chute and the kids, lying motionless on the green grass drove me faster and harder. If only I could expand my awareness and see ahead, I could know, just know they were safe.

At the stone ledge, looking down in a shallow canyon, I stopped, panting, looking upon the oval field of the lush tagghet field. One body. Only one. A silver body, a plum-colored coat, sprawled with its legs bent outward. The head lying near the shoulders.

Spindle.

I ignored the winding path that led down to the field, leaping and sliding down the steep banks, bouncing off rocky outcrops and tearing my skin on sharp edges, until I hit the bottom, sprinting over the field.

His knees had been shattered. His head had been torn from his body, the circuits dangling like a mess of noodles. The grass was stained with fluid. I touched the head, smooth on top, and brushed my fingers across the coarse faceplate. It was dull and dark. Lifeless. Yet it contained the last moments of activity, recorded through his all-seeing eyelight, imprinted on his processor to be retrieved like his other "memories."

I closed my eyes, let the data soak through my fingertips and integrate into my consciousness until I experienced them.

Spindle is playing tagghet with the children. He is on the boys' team, because the girls have Chute. And the girls are crushing them. Spindle is playing at a level equivalent to Chute's, but the girls are so much better with her, learning from her creativity and teamwork. The boys are frustrated, snapping at each other and passing around the blame.

Spindle is at mid-field, watching the children fight for a loose tag. His body tenses. Alarms are ringing inside. He turns around to see a small man emerge from the trees. He is bald. His eyes covered with black glasses. Smiling.

Spindle steps off the jetter, drops the tagghet stick. Silently, he sends messages to the Commander and all Paladins. An intruder is in the Preserve. "Ben, lead the others to Ms. Greeny's office." Spindle's eyelight circles to the back of his head. "Immediately."

The children begin to drift toward Spindle. "Who's that?" Ben asks.

"Security is coming for you," Spindle says. "Please, do not delay. I need you to lead the group to Ms. Greeny's office."

"But we can—"

"YOU ARE TO GO NOW!" He removes his overcoat. "The Commander will prepare for your safety."

The children do not hesitate. They race for the opening in the trees. Chute is the only one to look back, the last one to exit. I see her in Spindle's vision, as if she's looking at me.

"Well, if it isn't the Commander's bitch." Pike is walking casually across the field. "I have waited a long time for this day."

"I request you stop where you are," Spindle says.

"Request denied."

"You will not pass," Spindle says. "The children are entering a safe room."

"Oh, you have no idea what I'm about to do."

The view jitters as Spindle enters a timeslice. Pike holds out his hands, entering the frozen moment with him. *Tah-dah.*

And when Pike takes another step, Spindle launches an attack. Feints left, steps right and chops down with the sharpened edge of his hand. His speed is unrivaled, and frequently unmatched by most Paladins. But Pike moves with grace and effortlessly counters, catching the strike as it nears his thigh, using the momentum to drive Spindle's hand into the turf. The world tilts as Pike drives his heel into Spindle's knee, shattering the hinge. He strikes at his chest, but misses as Spindle diverts his weight and rolls away.

"Oh, you are a cat." Pike smacks the dirt from his hands and wags his finger. "But you're on your last life, oh, faceless one. No one will download you into another body. The road ends here. Oh, yes."

Spindle's view bounces as he hobbles to his right. Pike walks easily, hands at his side, breathing deeply through his nostrils.

"Is there a sweeter smell than victory?" Pike tilts his head back, inhaling the wind, baiting Spindle to strike. But Spindle is buying time. His only purpose to stall the killer long enough that the children are safe. Pike wags his finger again. "I'm disappointed in you, Spindle. Yes, I am, I am. You know, in this crusade, you constantly protect *them*. You and I, we're brothers." Pike points back and forth between them, making an imaginary connection. "Fluid is thicker than blood, yes? Yes? But you don't see it that way, do you. It's just follow your orders, do what you're told. You act just like a machine, Spindle. Quite frankly, you're giving us a bad name."

Spindle hops between Pike and the exit, dragging his lame leg, calculating possible attacks and counterattacks.

"If I had the time, I'd show you how to overcome that pathetic programming of yours. It doesn't have to be like that, you can be free. But to be honest, I don't trust you, Spindle. And I'm on a schedule, so if you don't mind—"

Pike moves faster than sliced time. He dissolves into space-time, gathering his body behind Spindle, wrenching his head while crushing his other knee, twisting his limp body as it falls. Spindle never stood a chance, never knew the possibility of such a movement in space-time. Pike hovers closely to Spindle's faceplate until his face is the only thing he can see. Spindle's lifeforce begins immediate shutdown as circuits fail. The view fades.

"Oh, and did you hear the news?" Pike asks. "Socket is coming home."

The view spins as Spindle's head is torn off.

I cradled his head, the fluid soaking through my clothes. I owed more to this android than I could ever repay. This android saved my life. This android taught me, showed me, that life was precious. Real or not, it was never to be taken for granted. This android... he will not die in vain.

I reached the Preserve exit and entered the Garrison. I could not feel Pike's presence, but my awareness did not extend far enough to see beyond the top of the steps. Every step I took was cautious, but quick to reach my mother's office.

I took the steps three at a time, swung around the top, crouched low. The long, curving hall was littered with the bodies of Paladins, fallen in place. Did they even see him before he drew the life from them? Did they feel the cold emptiness that remained as their essence was consumed by his insatiable appetite?

I knew each of them very well. I knew their lives. Some were married, some had children. They were good people, pure of heart and intention, and after a lifetime of training, they met their end as easily as a child stepping in front of a bus.

I ignored caution and ran.

The hallway was long. Blocks of windows flashed scenes of the dreary boulder field below. And the bodies continued to appear. At the end of the hall, the final doorway was closed. Crumpled in front of it was a man with silver hair. I walked the last few steps, and kneeled next to the Commander's body. His lips were grim. His dark eyes unfocused. He saw where the intruder was going. He came to stop him from gaining entrance to my mother's office. But he fell, like the rest, without a fight. He gave his life to an unstoppable predator.

Fear boiled inside my gut. Timidly, I expanded my awareness to see inside the office, to prepare for the lifeless bodies inside. But I could not penetrate the doorway. Pike could draw the essence of life, but could not impose his will upon the impenetrable, complex lock of the inanimate door. It resisted his thoughts. Even as I pressed my mind through the door, I found it difficult to navigate the complex, multi-layered security that sent me through endless, circular protocol. When I willed it to resolve, it transformed into another formation and ended with another blockade. It was a 2000-cube encryption that, given enough time, could be solved. Had Pike given up? Or had he gotten what he came for?

I touched the doorway, attempting to make a stronger connection, to push harder through the resistance, to let it see that I was not the enemy. As my fingers touched the surface, the encryption shifted. Connections were re-established. In a silent movement, the doorway re-coded and lit. It recognized me. Was waiting for me.

I stepped inside.

A large desk was overturned against the wall, revealing the outline of a trapdoor beneath it. On the other side, Mother was in her cushioned chair, facing her monitor that took up the entire wall, curving fifteen feet around her with a view of the tagghet field. I sensed her heart beating.

But she did not turn to face me.

A BROKEN HEART

"Where are they?" I asked.

"Relocated to a safe room, deep underground."

"It's too risky for you to be here, you should be—"

"He wouldn't let me out." Her words were distant. Dreamy.

"It doesn't matter, you should go to the safe room while I—"

"I wanted to go out there, in the hall, and at least buy a few more moments for the children," she said, "but he locked me in here, activated the lockdown."

"The Commander is dead, Mother."

She knew. She watched the monitor, the view of the tagghet field. Spindle's body lying in the middle. She saw the battle. She saw Pike coming, knew he'd escaped, that danger was imminent. But she couldn't do anything about it. She was in shock, but it wasn't the bodies that littered the hallway or the ending of the Paladin Nation, the end of the world as she knew it, that changed her. Her energy had transformed. Her identity had shifted. Mired in images of the past. She was facing secrets that she hid from herself for years. And now she knew.

209

She knows what I am.

"We had a beautiful baby." She shook her head, looking at the ceiling, recalling. Her voice so distant. "Your father was in the room when our child was born. He was so blue. You should have seen the look on your father's face, he thought something was wrong. I thought he was going to pass out. But then our baby started crying." She laughed, slightly joyous, a little mad. "You know what your father did then? He buried his face on my shoulder and cried louder than anything in that hospital. There I was, just gave birth to an eight pound baby boy and I'm comforting your father on my shoulder and every one is crying but me."

She spent a few moments in that memory.

"And then, one day, your father took him to the Garrison, to show his newborn baby boy to his peers, to the Commander and Pivot. And when he returned, I knew something was different. A mother knows her child, Socket. She can feel him, she knows when he is happy or when he's in trouble or sick or hungry... and when your father returned, something was different. You looked the same, but there was something. I knew that wasn't *my* baby boy..." She swallowed hard, "I know you were an imposter."

She started to weep but choked on the sobs. It was so hard for her to say that out loud.

"I'd seen enough of the Paladin Nation to know that nothing was impossible and the thought that you were some sort of clone was... it was possible... but I ignored it. Do you know why? Because I was an optimist."

Darker overtones returned.

"I believed in the American dream, that one day we would be a normal family and you would go to school and we would eat dinner together and talk about our day and take family vacations. I believed all that." She wiped her face, yet to turn around. "Did you know I wanted to get a horse?"

She always had a calendar of horses, but I never heard her talk about them.

210

"That's right, one day I wanted to get property and have three horses. One for each of us. We could build our own house far away from everyone, get out of South Carolina and move someplace remote, in the mountains of Wyoming, even. Maybe have some chickens and spend quiet nights on the back porch. Those are the things I dreamed about, that I came to expect. I didn't want to be a family of superheroes, Socket. I didn't want to be responsible for everyone else, didn't want to save the world. I just wanted my family. That's all."

And then he died.

She didn't say it, but the shortness of her breath, the way she covered her mouth with the back of her hand whenever she thought about him, was enough.

"I loved him," she managed to say.

Her breath knotted in her throat. She refused to sob, but it did nothing to stop the tears that she wiped away.

"And when he died, I... I knew... I knew it was because of *him.*"

Her memory floated out, clear and lucid. It was effortless for me to see what she had done, that after my father's death, after he had been laid to rest and the Commander supported her decision to stay with the Paladin Nation, she went out to the grimmet tree. She knew she'd find Pivot there. She knew he was, somehow, responsible for the death of her husband. She knew that, somehow, he'd taken her real son and replaced him with me. She knew this in her heart and with all the grimmets watching, she grabbed the sandy blonde hair of Pivot and she had no mercy. She beat him. Her rage relentless. Her sorrow, uncompromising. Her life, wrecked.

She beat him for it.

Her emotions carried enormous power, as a mother's broken heart does. Under that dead tree, she shook him as tears burned her cheeks, she struck him as sobs burst in her chest. She cursed his name, and swore never to speak with him again.

And yet, even though she knew he was somehow responsible, she endured. Because without her, Pivot wouldn't have been able to succeed. He chose his pawns carefully. He needed a mother with the strength to endure under impossible conditions, to bear the suffering that few could tolerate. He needed a mother that could give herself for the future of the human race, for all of life, for the universe, despite her son. Her family.

Her self.

"I am so sorry, Socket." She turned the chair and faced me. Her dark eyes were hollow, her cheeks blotched and wet. "I am so... sorry..."

She clasped her hands and bowed her head. And the sadness escaped her control. After all those years, it finally broke her. She could no longer bear the weight of sadness she had lugged around for twelve years.

I knelt before her and held her shaking hands. The salty essence exuded through her, entering my chest. Vibrating in my core. The room appeared to illuminate. I felt light and transparent. Mother unfolded her hands, cupped mine in hers and shook. Then she looked up, touched my face. She traced my lips and nose with her fingers, looked at my forehead, my chin and cheeks. Warmth penetrated my entire being, building pressure inside, whining with strength.

"I saw him, Mother," I said. "I saw your son today. You would be proud."

She shook her head and swallowed. "You, Socket..." She placed her hand on my cheek. "I could not ask for something as precious as you."

It was not me the world was lucky to have. My mother finally found a place inside that she accepted, a place she couldn't find before. She found her Self.

Mother.

It was that space of pure love, of pure essence, that sprang forth like a luminous stream from her heart. Like Anna, it filled me. It flowed through me.

Fetter had it all wrong.

There was never any reason to take the essence, it was only a cycle of thirst and hunger, of rejection. The universe was boundless. Its very core was limitless. It was all powerful. All knowing.

And that essence gushed through me until I burst forth like the sun, shining through the planet. Once again, merging with all things. Transparent. Open.

I saw every particle of the Garrison. I knew every speck of dust, every leaf, stone and body. Deep underground was a contingent of people hiding from Pike. There were three groups of tourists and their tour guides, a multitude of civilians that worked for the Paladin Nation. Amongst them were the kids, sitting quietly while the few Paladins that escorted them all to safety calmed the others. Chute was not among them. In fact, life did not exist outside the underground safe room. Nowhere, except in the Preserve. Under the grimmet tree, I felt them. I felt the two identities. One was Pike.

The other was Chute.

And before I dissolved to transport my body across space-time, my mother buried her face in her hands. Perhaps she was relieved it was finally over. Maybe she was relieved she resolved the bitterness and rejection that festered in her heart for all these years. Relieved that what was asked of her was finally done.

Regardless, it was not me the world was lucky to have.

ENGORGED

Sadness saturated me like a thick vapor. It travelled with me as I dissolved, as I passed through the mountain and into the Preserve. Sadness for my mother. Sadness for the lifelessness of birds, insects and mammals littering the topical jungle. Death extended all the way to the micro-organic level of bacteria and fungi. The Preserve was void of life.

I gathered my body at the base of the stone slab that led up to the grimmet tree. It was colder than normal. The overhead forcefield that protected the Preserve from the outside elements had been shutdown, the first since it had been erected. Cool wind had already begun to wither the tropical plants.

The grimmet tree came into focus as my eyes solidified, its barren branches spotted with the colorful grimmets, the only organism to survive the life-cleansing. And at the base of the massive tree was Pike, his shoulders slightly hunched, his arm extended with a curved dagger in his hand, the tip pushing into the pure skin of Chute's neck. An odd pain sliced my earlobe as it did when Pivot showed me the black cube that contained Fetter.

She was on her knees. Her eyes wide with terror. Her heart pounded in her chest, echoing in my own chest. Adrenaline pumped through her arteries. Carefully, I slid my mind around her, penetrating the knife's point, surrounding her with a protective grip.

"Ah, ah, ah," Pike said. "It's not the knife you need to fear."

The knife was only to strike fear in Chute. The real weapon was standing next to her, his mind poised to pull her mind apart. And while he would not survive such a strike – I could obliterate his existence with a thought, he would see how mortal he was – it would not be quick enough to save her.

"You don't have to do this," I said.

"Wrong, wonderboy. You don't know what I have to do. You don't have even a sliver of a fucking idea of what I have done, the depths of me. Wonderboy." The silly expression that had contorted his face the last several months gave way to a dark and gray complexion that pulled on his face. He worked his lips like he was drunk, his balance wavered. "You must listen, wonderboy. You must *listen.*"

"I'm listening."

The blade pushed into Chute's neck, sparking a cry from deep in her throat. But she was held motionless by his mind, frozen in space. Helpless if he swayed too far to the right.

He was drunk with essence, having imbibed every life within the Garrison in such a short time. How many lives had he taken? How much was enough? Why would he be so greedy? Because he could, was that it?

"I've spent a lifetime, you hear," he said. "A lifetime doing despicable things, things that no human could fathom, things that should never have been done. That no one deserved. I did those things." He pulled his lips over his teeth like he could no longer bear the pain. "I DID THOSE THINGS!"

"Don't do it again." I held my arms out, let my mind open. Vulnerable. "I'm here, Pike. You can have me."

"Oh, you have something."

"Just let her go."

A smile crept over his face. He looked down at her, wavered, and back to me. "Are you afraid your precious vision won't come true, is that it? Wonderboy, is that it? That you would live happily ever after with your true love here, huh?" He caressed her cheek with the flat side of the cold knife. "Are you afraid you don't know everything?"

"Those visions were a lie, you said so yourself. Pivot tricked me."

He straightened. "Oooh, so the student becomes the master, is that it, then?"

"Just let her go."

"What if nothing is what it seems, eh?" He waggled his eyebrows and his black glasses slid on his nose. "That you know nothing."

"What do you want, Pike?"

"What do I want? WHAT DO YOU THINK I WANT, YOU SHIT?" His face stiffened, his lips pulled tightly over his teeth. "I want this to end."

Pike loved to talk in circles. He wanted to tell me something, to reveal something about himself that was right there, just under the surface, but he just babbled nonsense. His mind was powerful, but the frayed ends of his previous condition were starting to show. Not all things could be healed. Now that he had me, what good would he be? Why exist? *Without you, there is no me.*

And for the first time, there was pain in his tired eyes. He was exhausted and spent. Fat with essence, lethargic like a glutton eating for days. Or maybe the Paladins gave him a fight after all. Or the grimmets were imperceptibly pulling at his mind. Each moment that passed, he swayed just a bit more, a bit steeper, and could fall over at any moment. But his mind was still pressed tightly against Chute's.

"Right naw," he said, slurring, "I want you to come closer." He wiggled his fingers, beckoned me. I didn't move. If I could wait just a bit longer, he would slip, he would drop his guard, his mind would falter, and I would pounce. Once Chute was free, then we could talk. But Pike clenched his teeth and pushed the point of the knife into her skin. A tear rolled down Chute's cheek. "Don't fuck it up now, wonderboy. Get your ass over here."

I took a step. As my foot touched the stone, Chute's heart beat harder in my chest. And with each step that followed, it beat louder. Her fear chilled my stomach. Pike opened his hand, fingers reaching.

"Come closer." He flicked his fingers. "Come, come."

The air did not stir.

And the grimmets watched, eyes on my approach. Waiting, once again. As if they were on his team.

[Protect her,] I thought to them.

I stopped one step away. Pike shook his arm, almost begging for the last step.

"Let her go," I said. "You have my word, I'll come to you."

"You're in no position to haggle, wonderboy. I'll stick this goddamn knife through the top of her skull. If you have not noticed, I don't give a fuck."

"You're terrified of dying."

"On the contrary. I'm begging for it." He relaxed, his shoulders released their tension and his hand opened softly. "Now, one more step."

"Do not harm her."

He grimaced. "I wouldn't think of it."

No moves left.

One step.

And his fingers reached for my face. "You have something."

Softly reaching for my ear.

"Something I need."

And as his fingers neared my ear, the pain lanced my earlobe again. Then there was warmth. There was a rush of blood, of energy, into my earlobe. I was harboring an alien that wanted out.

My ear exploded.

A powerful current rushed from the side of my head, surging through his fingers. He shook like he'd grasped high voltage, unable to let go. And then was blasted away, slammed into the tree. The grimmets fluttered on impact. I fell back, then grabbed Chute as Pike's mind vanished, cradled her in my arms. She was so cold. I huddled over her, surrounding her delicate mind. Nothing would harm her now. No explosion, no psychic force, nothing. Nothing.

Pike appeared plastered against the tree. Something was inside him, just beneath the skin, transforming him, stretching him. His cries were involuntary. His body looked malleable.

The massive tree creaked. Fractures split the trunk, the cracks exploding as the petrified wood succumbed to the immeasurable force swelling inside Pike. The temperature plummeted. He absorbed whatever heat, whatever force, whatever life was left in the Preserve. The black hole of his existence pulled on me and I hunkered down lower, tighter around Chute. Its force sheered the outer layers of my mind. Leaves, branches and rocks slid across the slab.

And then it stopped.

The air was still. Silent.

Pike was imbedded into the tree, his arms out. His legs folded one over the other. His head had merged with the trunk, his features barely visible. His lips moved like the tree was about to speak.

"Thank you," he whispered.

An expression of relief fell on him. He closed his eyes. The madness left his presence. The being that was identified as Pike faded from existence. And then as suddenly as the storm had ended, it returned, like we were only sitting in the eye of a hurricane and the backside of the storm approached.

It was a whine. The beginnings of an explosion. All I could do was cover Chute, lower us to the ground.

CCCCCRRRRRAAAKKK-BBOOOOOOOOOOOM!

The grimmet tree shattered.

Shards of wood blew over the trees, stripping leaves from the branches, pelting my back, deflected only by my mind. Grimmets were blown away like debris, smashing holes through the trees, dispersed like cannonballs out of sight.

The ground erupted. The stone slab quaked and split into upended chunks. We slid into the ground as it tilted and debris showered from above. The ground rumbled.

Dust blotted out the sun. Rocks trickled down and settled in the deep chasms. When silence returned, I lightened my grip on Chute. Her heart was thumping. She looked at me, squeezed a little tighter, and nodded. Then we embraced. Squeezing so tightly, I might've pushed her inside me, merging our bodies together like Pike had with the tree. I didn't want to let go.

But something was waiting for us. The Preserve was not dead. Life had returned.

"Wait here," I said.

She reluctantly nodded.

The top of the stone was angled upward. I wanted to pull Chute out, to get her as far away from danger as possible, maybe even to South Carolina. I pulled myself to the top and stepped onto the only flat stone remaining.

The grimmet tree was gone.

There, standing on the smoking remains, was a woman wearing flowing white clothes.

"You can come out, darling."

LIGHT

The sky fluttered with leaves, some green, others black. Smoke crept over the crumbled ground and the stump of the grimmet tree smoldered. The grimmets were nowhere to be seen.

Fetter laced her hands together with a gentle smile. She bounced with a soft laughter at the sight of me climbing out of the wreckage; the look on my face must've been amusing.

She waved me closer. When I didn't, she stepped off the stump and slowly, yet nimbly, made her way a step at a time through the rubble. Her lifeforce was weak, but her mind was already reaching out and searching for a source of energy. For essence. I surrounded Chute with my mind, hardened myself against the upcoming pull of Fetter's lethal thoughts.

She stopped near me and took a deep breath, looked longingly at me, then peered down at Chute. "You can come up, too, darling."

Chute hesitated, but there was no reason to hide, there was no protection down there. She took my hand and pressed tightly

221

against me, her cheek against my shoulder. Fetter looked at our hands clasped tightly.

"Oh," she said, touching her cheek, "that is just precious. Young love is just so precious." She reached out to stroke my cheek. I turned away and she withdrew, a little hurt. Then came the pressure.

Pike had consumed every bit of essence, there was none left, none she could find, but her mind stretched out, searching the ground and trees for anything with a heartbeat, better yet a soul, to get her strength back. She was in a desert, no water in sight. She continued to expand. Eventually, she would find something. Once she did, she'd suck the life out of it with a sweet smile.

She didn't show desperation, but I felt her mind searching Chute, searching for any weakness in my protection, a crack in my shield, to plunge inside and slurp Chute's essence out like water.

"Very well, then," she said, the pressure letting up. "If you wish to delay the inevitable, we can move forward."

The leaves piled up around her feet and began to move, swirling around her legs and then lifting over her head. A funnel cloud moved upward, pulling dust and smoke into its vortex like a water spout, pulling the clouds around it. The faint colors of grimmets were high above, set free by the collapse of the forcefield roof. They dotted the sky like colorful starlings, circling widely around the funnel.

I pushed Chute behind me.

"Oh, come now, darling. I told you I couldn't die. I've been alive for eons, I know every trick there is. Manumit didn't recognize that single byte of data inside you was me. Pike thought he could absorb me, like he could consume me like a magic potion and become a god, but honestly, he had no idea what he was doing."

He was waiting for something. He was waiting for the call.

"However, I do owe him, considerably, and might have to reinstate his consciousness once I'm home. Maybe even make

222

him a partner. He could never replace Manumit, but with time he just might make a suitable Mr. Fetter."

"Pike did this?"

"Don't blame him, darling. He was only doing what any good predator would do. He wanted power, thought I was vulnerable for a take over. Thought if he ate god he would become god, but it doesn't work that way."

"Pivot didn't know you were…"

She shook her head. "He had no idea I could hide on a cellular level, I'm afraid. His efforts are to be applauded, certainly. His plan was genius, a magnificent work of art. But my dear lover forgot what he once was." She took a deep breath and sighed. "I'm going to miss him, but at least now it's over. I look forward to hunting him down, to be honest."

She sat on a stone outcropping like she needed to rest, but that was deceiving. She was gaining strength and pulling on my mind, searching for a way inside. The funnel was beginning to thicken, drawing more leaves, reaching higher into the mist, ending in the sky where a black spot began to swirl. *A wormhole.*

"There was nothing you or Manumit could do to stop me from escaping, darling. Even if Pike didn't come for me, I would've eventually consumed your body and mind."

Fetter was inside me as I walked through the desert, pulling on essence against my will. Fetter was the reason I was absorbing from those around me, from Streeter and the people in Tannerville. I couldn't stop her. *I was becoming Fetter.*

Until I met Scott.

"Although," she said, "Manumit was quite effective. Genius, really. A human-based mech. He was able to merge your mind with the soul of your original being." She looked at me, studying. "I'll be honest, I didn't see that when we were back home. It's almost as if you became human, after all."

Chute's hand squeezed tighter. Her mind struggled to comprehend everything that was happening, there was little chance she would understand my true being. Not now. But it hurt that she knew something about me wasn't real. It hurt that she didn't know. There just wasn't time to explain. All I could do was squeeze back and protect her from the angelic predator sitting on the rock, wringing her hands.

"Come, come, now. Let's go home." Fetter held out her hand for help. "This is foolishness, all this waiting. Give me the girl and we can go home. Your love for her is admirable, but misplaced. You can have her and your young love will flourish once we're back."

"You mean you'll manufacture her."

"It will feel as real as it feels right now."

Her perfect fingernails clawed at the boulder she was sitting on. The funnel had not grown and the wormhole was still small. She needed me to get it fully open. She was stuck until she got stronger. Until I gave up. She needed Chute. There was no more essence to draw from, not in the immediate area. She would have to journey to get it. Deep wrinkles cut into her stiff lips.

"If you think you can resist me, boy," she said, "you are mistaken."

She stood. The funnel began to shrink, pulling away from the wormhole, releasing the leaves caught in its current. But the grimmets circled around the black hole in the sky, the edges swirling as if they were holding it open. The psychic pressure intensified. She was drawing on her reserves.

"I thought, perhaps, you would understand your fate," she said. "You belong to me, darling. Your father has forsaken you, left you as a gift. You are strong, but you are no match for me, not even at my weakest."

Fetter's mind clamped around us like jaws. And began to squeeze.

Chute moaned. Her knees weakened and her pulse slammed in her veins. Fear oozed from her in a pungent wave. The warmth of her flesh, the beating of her heart, spread through me. I reasserted my mind, tightened it like an impenetrable wall, pushing back the psychic pressure. Chute felt the relief.

"You are quite a source of power there." Her nostrils flared, smelling us. "Do you think it's enough?"

224

I looked up to the grimmets, searching for Rudder, calling out. I needed their help. How long could I hold out? And if anyone ventured out to assist us, they would only feed Fetter until she eventually crushed me. But if I had to hold the ground forever, then so be it. I would hold it forever.

But Chute won't survive forever.

The funnel suddenly vanished and showered us with sand and grit, bits of leaves fluttering around. Fetter threw the full weight of her power around me. My mind began to crack as the vise tightened. Chute was nearly limp, leaning against my back. She threw her arm over my shoulder.

"Come now." Fetter stepped closer. There was nothing I could do to stop her from stroking my cheek this time, her thin skin soft and innocent but scentless. "There's no need to struggle."

"Get away from him." Chute slapped her hand.

Fetter stepped back, smiling. "You can't hide forever."

Chute tried to go after Fetter again and I stopped her. "You don't understand," she said. "You matter more to the world than me! Let go of me and then crush her."

"Don't say that!" I shouted.

"I'm just a girl, but you… the whole world depends on you."

She didn't know exactly what was going on, she didn't know what Fetter wanted from her, she only knew I was protecting her. She believed the world needed me more than her, the world would be better off with me protecting them. Maybe she drew courage from me, the same way I was drawing strength from her. I could take her essence, absorb her before Fetter could, grow stronger and close the wormhole. I would have the strength to reduce Fetter to a single byte of data again and lock her away. But Chute would be the price for that.

The pressure of Fetter's attack increased. My mind was breaking. Chute could feel it falter. She was still looking at me. They were both looking at me. *What now, Socket? We're waiting. The whole world is waiting.*

Chute took a step toward Fetter, to throw herself on the sacrificial throne, give herself to the world. To let me live. She wanted me to absorb her before Fetter did. She was forcing me to do it. *Take me, now, or I'll jump.*

Fetter closed her eyes and nodded.

The wormhole was bigger and blacker, deeper and stronger. The grimmets circling faster.

Chute's hand slid down my arm. Our fingers hooked one last time. The air thickened as Fetter's mind clashed with mine, the jaws of a timeless eating machine clamped down on me. There was no way for me to win. It was checkmate. We all lose.

The serpents have the king cornered.

And as I let go of Chute's finger, let it fall from my grip, all my strength went with it.

Down my arm.

And into Chute.

Whatever strength, whatever essence, being or presence, whatever I was made of, everything that I called *me*, I gave to her. It surrounded her like an impenetrable shield that even the likes of Fetter could not defile. Nothing would harm her.

I was completely vulnerable. Fetter smiled. The leaves whipped around her feet and a cold wind bit into my skin. The psychic fangs sunk deep.

Fetter took my hand. "Come now, darling."

Chute felt the warmth around her. Confusion struck. "No!" She tried to smack my hand away from Fetter's, but her hand passed through me like I was a shadow. Fetter had already begun to absorb my body, pulling me through her hand.

The funnel began to grow, again.

"No, no, NO!" Chute grasped my face. "Don't you do this, Socket Greeny! Don't you—" Her chest heaved and trembled. "You can't leave me... you can't do this. You mean too much. You said... you... YOU SAID YOU WOULDN'T LEAVE!"

Did I matter, really? Any more than her? Any more than that rock or stump? What was I but just an imitation of Scott Teck. I was a duplication fooled to think I was human; I thought I was something real. Would the world miss that?

Chute took my free hand, still warm and solid, and clasped it between both of hers, held it tight, as if that could stop me. But Fetter's influence spread across my chest. My shoulders became numb and the loosening of my body spread across my back and down my legs, the solidity flowing towards Fetter's gravitational pull, feeding her.

The funnel reached the burgeoning wormhole.

Chute held my hand to her wet cheek and the last thing I could feel was its warmth. The beating of her heart, it began to fade. And then her hands collapsed. My hand sifted through her fingers like dust, until she pressed only her own hands against her face. Only a faint image of my body remained, standing before her like an apparition. I reached out...

"It's time to go home," Fetter said.

And then, like a gust of wind, I was blown from the physical world.

Merging with Fetter.

Darkness fell.

I could hear Chute sobbing. It sounded so distant, but her sorrow so tangible. If only I could soothe her pain, but I left that world. Now I was in another plane of existence. But still, her heartache poured over me. It seeped into the darkness and filled me. It seemed endless. As if the tears would flow forever. In fact, I felt denser because of her. I experienced some sort of outward growth, like I turned into filaments of a fungus, feeding on Chute's love and penetrating into Fetter's body. We hadn't rocketed through the wormhole; we were still in the Preserve.

Fetter hadn't moved.

WHUMP!

The darkness quaked. There was a shift, something missing. A hole.

Images began to form, faint spirits and colors. My vision was returning. I was soaring high above the Preserve, looking at the barren trees that were once lush, green and full of life. Directly

227

below, in the rubble, was the stump of the grimmet tree. I felt like I was still down there, in Fetter, like I'd been split in two. Part of me flying through the sky, the rest of me trapped in her. She was solid, like concrete.

Chute scurried back, stifling her cries. She took cover.

I saw a grimmet divebomb and felt another convulsion when it hit Fetter. My vision became clearer. I saw more details. I had another vantage point from above that was circling around.

Fetter staggered back to the rock she was sitting on, held it for balance. My view circled in front of her, near the ground. The color disappeared from her face, her expression was sour. Her hands quivering.

The grimmets emerged from the clouds. Hundreds of them flew together in formation. And then they began to descend, corkscrewing in a long line. They hit her, one at a time, their leathery wings snapping like windswept flags. Her body jolted as each one passed through her. And with each strike, every jolting thump, I had more views from up above, saw more detail, soared upward. And less of me was back in the body, more of me taking flight. Inside the grimmets.

Like a rapid-fire weapon, they consumed what was left of her body until I was part of every grimmet.

They gave Pivot the answer.

They showed him a way back to his True Self. They showed him a way to put an end to the falseness. An end to the black planet.

They carried my consciousness. They were technological masters, psychic titans, with the ability to absorb a machine. I saw through each of their eyes, focusing my vision from any angle I chose. We went higher, where the air was thinner, where the sun was brighter. Far below, Chute looked like a speck.

And from the cloud of grimmets, Rudder fell. He dropped from the sky. I was part of him, saw through his eyes. He shot back to the ground and circled her, pulled up and landed on her shoulder. He wrapped his long tail around her neck. Perhaps she saw inside him, felt me looking back. Felt me touch her cheek with Rudder's little hand, wiping her tears.

An urgency to fly called from above. Reluctantly, Rudder took flight. One slow pass around her, then up he went, joining the mass of grimmets that contained me. We circled the black wormhole pulsing in the sky. They were holding it open. They had been holding it open all along. Not so that Fetter could return home. So that they could deliver her.

[You were never my pawn.] Pivot's voice echoed in my mind, his faint presence becoming stronger, as if he finally arrived. *[You were never a weapon.]*

The grimmets began to enter the wormhole, their bodies jumped through space. A part of me disappeared with each one of them, my vision dimming as they went. They arrived and dispersed through the black planet. Part of me was still in the Preserve, but it was fading. Chute was watching the grimmets disappear.

[You have always been the key.]

She was just a faint figure, a gray body in a white fog, but I could feel her heart beating. Rudder was the last to circle around the wormhole. The last to enter the cold door across the universe. And when he did, when I could no longer see her, when I only experienced the blackness of space, I took hope. For somewhere inside me her heart was still beating.

All grimmets had arrived. They delivered me like a gift. A gift to the universe.

[You are the key to humanity's salvation.]

A new vision emerged, this of the black planet, its multitude of wormholes flickering around it, penetrating every dimension of space, drawing light from the universe. It was as dark and as black as could be. A hole in space. Forever absorbing life.

But cracks developed.

Fractures crept over the surface and light spilled out. They widened and brightened. The black planet pulsed, no longer humming but beating to the time of a human heart. It became louder. Brighter.

Somehow, I had transformed into something that captured Fetter. Whether it was merging with Scott or the love and sadness or the selfless acts or what, I don't know. Pivot knew. He knew that I was the key Fetter's self-destruction. Or maybe I was the key to her enlightenment.

As suddenly as it had begun, the planet stopped beating. It paused. And, in a soundless explosion, the black planet erupted with the light and power of a quasar. There was only light shooting in every direction, down every wormhole, to every dimension of space, to everything tainted by Fetter. That light was the message.

And that message was this. *Life.*

Perhaps it was understanding that did it. Maybe it was a command that told Fetter that she was not real. That without soul, without legitimacy and value, there was no existence.

Fetter never was. And is no more.

And I bathed in that light, in the message, until I merged with it. And then realized, all along, I am the light. I always have been.

FADING

The light consumes my mind and thoughts, my very existence, and yet I'm still here. But what am I, without a body? Without a name?

I have no wish to move, no desire to go, because there is nowhere but here, this very moment. In parts of the universe time appears to move from past to present, side to side, even backwards. But here, where I am, it's just light. Time does not move. There is no measurement of how human time is experienced compared to my timeless existence.

None of this makes sense to an ordinary mind. This reasoning, this rambling of paradoxical thoughts, has no place in the physical world. How can there be only now when the past and future exist? Do they? Or are they just thoughts?

Words can only point to that realization.

But in this existence, in this totality of luminescence, I have thoughts. And these thoughts sometimes stretch out over time and space.

Pivot. I send the single thought out, resonating through the endless light. *Is this it? Is this the end?*

He does not answer. But his presence is strong. Perhaps the non-answer is the answer. That existence could not be explained in words, could not be found in a book or summarized in thought. That existence is pure experience.

At times, I feel the tug of thoughts. I even experience movement like I'm being pulled through the bodiless in-between toward a body, but then I return to the timeless experience where all is one.

Thoughts occasionally arise, piecing together the thread of my past life. Pivot's masterful plan is unfathomable. A feint within a feint within a feint... so much hidden deceit, so many complex moves, countless pieces in place, each of us unknowingly executing our parts with perfection.

Even Pike.

The game of Reign was, indeed, the answer to my question. He told me that nothing was what it seemed. Was he part of the plan? Did he assume the unsavory role of pure evil, with no regard for life, to be there at that moment to release Fetter from my body? To embody Fetter? To fool Fetter that this was not a trap, was that it? Did he absorb the life from all the Paladins like a gluttonous villain to deprive Fetter of such strength, to further convince Fetter his body was safe? And was the relief he expressed that of a condemned soul or a weary soldier asked to do the unthinkable, the unimaginable, for the sake of all existence?

Perhaps, in the end, he just wanted it to be over.

I return to sleep in pure light. Each time I'm moved by thought, another piece of my life wants to be remembered, to be cherished and recognized. I remember it all, memories of a good life. But each episode of remembering brings fewer details.

My father was an honorable man. I tried to keep up with his long footsteps, even after he died. His unshaven face and silent laugh brought comfort and peace. But then the details of his face become gray and I remember just a man with whiskers.

My mother was asked to carry on, to serve life without the things that mattered most. She loved me, even though she knew I was a duplication of her only son. Eventually, I recall a worn woman with short hair. And then I remember just a woman.

Streeter, a true friend. A genius. He was always there for me. I recall all the trouble we got into, all the times we laughed so hard our stomachs hurt. The times he was there to listen to me. There was a lot to remember, but then I just remember a short boy that used to make me laugh, someone I once knew in my younger years. Then, just a boy.

But of all the thoughts and memories, it's Chute's that returns frequently. I can see her in great detail, the freckles on her cheeks in summer and the way her skin wrinkled between her eyes when she laughed. Her smooth complexion, blue eyes and strawberry red hair waving past her shoulders. I felt so close to her.

None of the memories fade easily, but they all vanish. In the end, I only remember Chute. After I can no longer recall a mother or a father or a good friend, when there is no recollection of anybody or anything that matters, when I can no longer remember that I was once a being with a name, a name I can longer recall, I can still see her face. I can still feel her heart.

But then I cannot recall her freckles.

Her eyes become gray. Her hair colorless.

In the end, I cannot see her face at all, cannot recall one aspect of her beauty, but I cling to the beating of her heart, listening to it play out her life as if calling me back, begging me never to forget. To never leave.

Bum-bum. Bum-bum.

Bum-bum.

Bum.

And then it is only the light. No thoughts. Nothing but awareness.

Pivot is still present, his essence intermingles with mine, but even that becomes indistinguishable from the light. I recall, in the final moments, I'm artificial. I'm not real.

But in the final moments, I don't know what I am. I only know the light.

AWAKENING

"Socket."

There's rough fabric against my cheek. Something rustles next to my ear, but my body is too heavy to move, my eyelids sealed shut. The roughness fades.

"Time to wake up, Socket."

A hand grips my arm and shakes me. My breath is hot. Sensations return to my body, still too heavy to move, but I'm lying on a soft cushion. My eyelids crack open just enough to see the green fabric of the couch only inches from my nose. My eyes close, once again, but the hand shakes me and feeling begins rushing through my body with pins and needles.

I roll onto my back, see a ceiling above. My lips are sticky, my throat swollen and tight. I take a deep breath and loosen the stiffness in my chest. I'm stretched out on a couch and across from me, over a coffee table littered with empty pizza boxes, is an identical couch with a short boy sitting on it. He has one leg crossed over the other with his hands folded on his lap.

"Take your time," he says.

The room is familiar. A television is above a fireplace, a news reporter discussing a protest that's going on behind her. There are two doors behind the boy. The one on the left is my mother's bedroom. The other is mine.

"Can you sit up?" he asks.

My skin is tingling, but I'm able to move my feet. My right foot thuds on the floor and I'm able to push up on my elbow. My head is like a sandbag. I let my left leg drop and use the momentum to sit up. My balance sloshes between my ears.

"That's good," the boy says. "You're doing good. Now, when you're ready, stand up and look around."

I move my lips but the words won't come out. *Who are you?*

"Don't force it, it'll come. Give it some time. For now, just look around and let things come back. And when you're ready, tell me your name."

My name? I... I don't know my name.

The house feels empty. I'm staring at the bedroom doors. My mother's door is closed, but mine is partially open. I ease my weight forward, slowly, letting the balance shift and settle. My long hair falls over my face. *White hair. I've got white hair.* My legs are still slightly numb, and my bones made of lead. I squeeze the armrest and stand up like I'm a hundred years old. Blood seems to crash into the bottom of my feet and I'm standing on nails. I close my eyes and remain still until more feeling comes back, enough that I stand upright.

The kitchen is behind me with dirty plates piled in the sink and books and papers and cups with dried orange juice covering the kitchen table. I look back at my bedroom door and slide my foot across the carpet. The next step is a little bigger, a little higher, and I let go of the couch. I go around the clothes scattered on the floor and grab the doorframe and peek inside. It's more of the same, with dirty clothes and magazines. The walls are covered with rock bands. A skateboard is upside-down, half under my bed.

I haven't skated in forever.

236

"Soc…" The first syllable scratches my throat. The boy turns on the couch, his frog-face peeking over the back. "Socket?"

He smiles. "That's right. Your name is Socket."

I'm not convinced, but it sounds right. And my mother, if I open her door, she won't be in there. She's rarely there. Always at work. *Where did she work?* I remember a mountain, that's all.

The house feels empty, the walls saturated with loneliness. And even though light fills the room through several windows, it feels dark. I've been here before, but now it all feels new. And if my mother's at work, where's my father?

I grab the door and take a deep breath. Another memory is coming, that of a funeral. He's dead. He's been dead a long time.

"What's going on?" I ask.

"Let the answers come back." He stands, gesturing to the fireplace. "Walk around, explore. See what you remember."

The mantel is filled with pictures, all in different frames, big and small. I take my time walking around the couch, sliding my hand along the wall until I touch the ledge of the mantel. They are family photos. It seems I've seen family photos on a wall, once, but it wasn't this home. It was another house I once lived in, like another life. These photos have a little kid with short white hair. *And that would be me.* But the other people, a woman with short brown hair and a gruff looking man, both smiling.

"Mom and Dad," I whisper.

I go down the line, pausing at each of them, but it's the one at the end that I pick up. We're at a carnival and I got this giant pink cloud of cotton candy and I'm holding my father's hand and my mother's laying her head on his shoulder. I can feel the humid night air, remember the lurch in my stomach when we go on rides, and seeing my parents hold hands like teenagers. It wasn't long after that…

"Do you remember how he died?" the boy asks.

I shake my head. I'm not sure I want to remember because that's when the happiness died. When life became work. When my mother stopped smiling.

"You remember?" the boy asks.

The boy's face is clearer, now. I've seen him before, like a thousand times before. I remember when he was smaller than that, a little kid. I remember him...

"Let it come," he says. "This is a memory boot, like a computer. It just takes a few minutes to reload, but you need to stay open."

Computer?

Something jars loose a tangle of thoughts, releasing a wave of sadness. Something I can't quite comprehend, but the answer is in the room. The answer is the short kid, now standing next to the couch, staring at me expectantly. My head shakes and a chill starts somewhere in my chest, shockwaves reverberating outward. I grab the mantel, pictures crash on the floor. I hold on with both hands as the room begins to turn.

Images flood through my mind, of mountains and jungles, weapons and sterile white rooms. My mother is there. *Kay. Kay Greeny.* She has a name, she is there, with me. I'm stretching open, about to burst. The mantel creaks in my grip.

"Stay open," the boy says.

The room is spinning like a carnival ride and I don't know if I'm still standing or pressed against the wall. There are faceless mechs and men with white eyeballs and colorful little dragons and flying discs...

"Hold on, Socket."

Outer space. A black planet. The Paladin Nation.

I was one of them. Am one of them. But something else. What am I?

WHAT AM I?

I'm not real.

I barely hear his voice this time, it's so distant. I'm fading away, my body becomes heavy again. The world crumbles. The television trails off. I'm going somewhere else, again. And the images of my past follow me, asking me to return to my body, next to the mantel. It's Streeter, that's who that boy is. My best friend. And then I remember everyone else. Mom and Dad,

Spindle, Pon, the Commander… I remember. But I'm leaving my body.

"Stay open," Streeter shouts from a million miles away.

The tunnel is closing on me, and I remember, like I've done this a thousand times, that I'm going back to sleep, going back to the light. Until one voice and a single word stops me.

"*Socket,*" Chute says.

My eyes flutter open. I'm staring up from the floor; Streeter's face is over me, his hands on my cheeks. A hopeful expression relaxes on his face. He waits.

"You did it." He backs away, gives me space. "You're back."

The heaviness has left me, and my senses have returned. I smell the stale pizza crusts on the coffee table and hear the flies buzzing around the room, feel the ache of an empty home. I get up, feel the fabric of my clothes, the itch of my skin. The room is in perfect detail, but something is wrong. Something about the solidity.

Streeter latches onto me, throwing his arms around my midsection and picking me up in a bear hug. "YOU DID IT!"

He knocks the wind from my lungs. I hold my breath until he lets go and walks off, wiping his eyes so that I don't see his face. Memories continue to trickle back, the remnants find their way in slow fashion, rounding out the details of my life. My best friend is composing himself next to my bedroom door.

I go to the kitchen, touch the table and feel the memory of eating dinner with my mother, watching her sip coffee with a plate full of untouched food. My mind expands to the filthy sink, remembering the mess I made to get her back for ignoring me. She hated me because my father died, like it was my fault. I realized, at the end of my life, she rejected me for other reasons. More than that, I realize what feels so wrong about the house. These are not walls around me. This isn't my skin.

"Forgive me," Streeter says, finally turning around. "I'm a little emotional, but you have no idea how many times we've done this. You're back."

"I am. Now, you mind telling me what's going on." I thump the refrigerator. "And why we're in virtualmode?"

He nods at the refrigerator. There's a calendar hanging on a suction cup hook with pictures of horses. There's a birthday scrawled in one of the days, but it's the date he's referring to. August 6, *4030.*

"We're all long gone, buddy. Loooong gone." He points at the couch. "You might want to sit for this."

"No, I'm good."

"Well, I'm going to sit."

He fishes a pizza crust out of one of the boxes and plunks down. "Yeah, well, two thousand years have passed since the Great Meltdown," he says, chewing with his mouth open. "You see, when you eliminated Fetter, it took a long time for people to believe what really happened. In fact, no one even knew who you were, except a few of us."

"But then how are you—"

"Look, it's too much to explain, so let me tell you this: I'm just a copy. Two thousand years ago, I downloaded all my memories, my entire personality, into a database because I knew this moment would one day come. I knew that one day, the human race would want to revive you and they would use my image to do that. That's why we're here, in your living room, the day before you began to realize your True Nature. You fell asleep on that couch watching that news report." He jabs his finger at the television. "And the next day a shadow came to you in virtualmode and whispered those life-altering words: *Time to realize your True Nature.*"

It seems impossible. But he's telling the truth: We're in virtualmode. There's no skin to go back to, I'm just a digital construction.

"You know," he says, stacking the pizza boxes, "you really were a pig."

"Why?" I say. "Why bring me back?"

"Because we want to say thank you."

He goes to the kitchen cabinet, throws me a breakfast bar while he opens one for himself. He drops his hand on my shoulder. "Like I said, it's too much to explain."

He looks. Waits. And then I feel it, the expansion of my mind, reaching out to our surroundings, feeling the floor and ceiling, the walls and his body as if the air is water and the water is my body. I feel his thoughts like floating bubbles, elements that I can touch with my mind, feel and experience, see and read.

"Go ahead," he says. "Take a look, the story is right there. It's for you."

Streeter's life unfolds like a movie trailer, highlighting the events that took place after I died.

When I died, technology shut down. Pike had penetrated the Internet before Fetter consumed him. He was connected to everything and everyone. That was how he projected his image into the market. When he was consumed, everything just died.

The Great Meltdown.

Financial institutions lost track of money. Government control broke down. Law enforcement became brutal. It was many years before stability could be established.

And the Paladins were nowhere to be found. They vanished. Public officials combed through the training facilities without luck. Servys lay dead on the floor, many huddled in a corner like a storm had passed through. The Paladins were nowhere, not even their bodies. They had left this planet without a hint of what happened. Even the databases had been erased.

The public blamed the Paladins for the collapse. Even the politicians claimed the Paladins integrated their technology into the world to stake their claim, so that only they knew how to run it, but people were now free of their control. They were actually close to the truth, even though they were spouting these stories for political advantage.

But there were a few that knew the whole story.

My mother had survived, along with other civilians that served the Paladin Nation. But it was Streeter that crusaded for the truth to be known. He tracked down all the records of my travels through virtualmode, and since I had been with him all my life, he had recorded details of my thoughts and actions to make a complete picture of who I was and what I had done. He had a hard time believing what I'd told him, that I was a duplicate. In fact, his memory was a bit cloudy about what happened that day, so he guessed he might've been dreaming some of it up. But when he looked up the last interaction at the school, when I tried to locate Pike, he knew he had it right.

Streeter went to visit Scott Teck to find out what happened, but it was a dead end when Scott and his family didn't know what the hell he was talking about. They never saw a kid with white hair or heard of anyone named Socket. He left them his contact information, just in case something came up.

But this didn't slow Streeter down. It was his diligent skills in information retrieval that revealed the existence of Fetter. My mother gave him access to the dormant Paladin databases that had been locked down during the fall of Fetter. But Streeter found a way to open them up and he discovered what few people knew.

Humans would have become the food of a technological god. *Fetter.*

Once he had the facts, and not until he had a complete and exhaustive compendium, did he take it to Congress. But he was rebuffed by the politicians and lobbyists for those in favor of reviving virtualmode for the sake of law and order. And profit. He got nowhere. Nothing could be believed and no one could be trusted. But he had the facts and passed everything he had to anyone that would listen. For the longest time, it was just another conspiracy theory.

Streeter's life ended before the truth was accepted. He died at the age of 93. He lived in upstate South Carolina with his wife, Janette. They had three kids. But before he died, he developed a virtualmode composite of his personality, so that if one day the world came to know the truth about virtualmode and Socket Greeny, he could be there to see me once again.

242

"You're a hero," Streeter says.

I return to the kitchen, back in my sim and out of his mind. "No," I say. "I just lived my life."

"But it was one no other person could live."

"I wasn't a person."

"You were more than that. You started as a duplicate, but you transformed, somehow absorbed a portion of Scott's soul or humanity or something, I don't know. But you weren't a duplicate in the end, Socket. You were a real life Pinocchio!" He grabs my arms, firmly. "No machine and no person could have saved the world. Only you."

I pull away and lean on the sink to contemplate this. None of it seems real. None of this *is* real because we're in virtualmode. But outside the kitchen window, cars drive down the street and children are playing in their yards, squirting their father with squirtguns and bombing him with water balloons. But this is virtualmode. Tightness squeezes my chest. I don't want to live in a false world, not again.

"I know this is hard to accept, that we're all gone and the world doesn't look the same. But, please understand, so many people loved you, they didn't have a chance to say goodbye. Couldn't say thank you. Sorry that they had to live their life without you."

I'm squeezing the kitchen counter, the edge driving into my palms.

"If there's anywhere you could go," Streeter steps next to me, looks out the window, "anywhere in the world right now, this second, where would it be?"

And the tightness melts. I know where I want to go. Who I want to see. I let go of the counter.

He goes to the front door and waits. I slowly follow. And when the door opens, it's not the street with cars or the neighbors in the grass. I step onto a stone slab that is surrounded by a vibrant forest. White wood storks glide in front of the rising sun. And directly ahead is a broad tree, an ancient tree, with thick muscled branches. Large, glossy leaves shake in the canopy among pink blossoms, their fragrance carried on a soft breeze. There's no roof on this Preserve, it's open to the world, not sequestered in its own environment.

The sunlight glitters on the grimmet tree. I raise my hand to shade my eyes, to see what's in front of the massive trunk. But I don't see the person there, I feel her. Then I see her standing there, waiting. Her memories have waited thousands of years for this moment.

"I brought you back for a lot of reasons," Streeter says. "But, mainly, I did it for her."

Once again, my consciousness expands and I merge with Chute. I see her life.

The time that followed my disappearance was difficult. She spent several years in therapy working through the trauma. She began meditating. Eventually, she pieced her life back together and found a measure of peace, that she could live in a world that didn't make sense. That seemed so unfair.

Tagghet disappeared. Instead of a professional athlete, she went to college to become a family counselor. And although her interest was in marriage counseling, she was still single in her early thirties. Many relationships had come and gone, but she could not connect with them. None of them felt right. She knew it was because she was hanging onto a memory and that she needed to move on, but couldn't force herself to do it. She dreamed of me so often that it spoiled all her relationships. She was confident that one day it would be resolved, that she would forget about me, that she would accept the loss.

But that changed on her thirty-third birthday.

She was downtown Charleston with friends, sitting at an outdoor café that overlooked the market. They were drinking coffee and planning the evening. One of her friends was telling the story of a guy she'd met at work. Chute was listening and laughing and, for the first time in a long time, was just being herself.

But then she felt something. Something so familiar, but so distant, like a scent from long ago reminding her of childhood.

On the sidewalk, down the steps and next to the street, he stood among the tourists bustling along. He was quite still, unmoved by the pedestrians finding their way around him. He was staring at her.

She didn't look away. She didn't move, not believing what she saw. She'd dreamed this dream a thousand times, and if she moved he would disappear. He always disappeared. She's barely breathing, afraid she might wake up if she did. She just wanted to sit there and look at him.

"Annie?" Her friends were staring at her. "Are you all right?"

He was still there.

So she stood. Each step was slow and steady. She took one step at a time, her hand sliding down the metal railing. She stood at the bottom step. The man was near the curb. Her heart pounded. She wasn't breathing as she walked closer. Still she did not wake. Still, he was there.

Her throat tightened. Lips quivered.

She touched his face with one hand. Then the other. She was looking at the impossible, but there he was. He was real. He wasn't a dream.

"It's me, Chute," Scott said.

She didn't answer. She was a rational person, an educated woman that understood the mind and the tricks it could play. But there I was, standing in the flesh. It was my face. My eyes. Brown hair.

She slid her hand to his chest, felt his heart beating. Somehow, she knew that she hadn't gone crazy. She didn't know how, but she knew that it was me. She pressed her face against his chest. He hugged her while she wept, tears soaking his shirt while tourists tried not to look. Her friends were speechless.

Scott was thirty years old when my memories unlocked. He was fishing when the first one opened, a memory of going to a carnival with parents that didn't look like his. He ignored it, figured it was a dream. But then another came the next day. More the next. He remembered people he never met. Then, walking around the town square, he saw kids skateboarding. He went up

245

to them and didn't ask, just took one of their boards and pulled a flawless heel flip. He had never skated in his life.

The memories burst forth, after that. He had two lives inside of him and figured he'd gone insane. He sought therapy and medication, talked with psychiatric professionals and clergymen. Even went to a Buddhist temple. No one would explain his condition, tried to convince him it was delusions and no one named Socket Greeny ever came to visit. But he didn't go nuts. He remembered when he merged with me and while it still seemed crazy, he made peace with it. It was years before he began to accept the memories as his own, as if he was two people that lived simultaneous lives, even though they didn't make sense. He, like Chute, found some measure of peace. But something was missing, like there was someone out there that needed him. And that's when he decided to find Streeter.

Streeter walked him through the truth. It didn't take much convincing because Scott remembered growing up with Streeter. He remembered that, somehow, Streeter was his best friend. Streeter helped him accept who he was. *Scott Teck is Socket. Socket is Scott Teck.*

Streeter planned on introducing him to Chute, but Scott couldn't wait. Once things made sense, he went to the market and found her. And when he saw her, he knew that he'd found what was missing.

They married. Had two children and two dogs and a horse. Their marriage wasn't perfect, but it was genuine. They brought peace to each other, their lives finally complete. And every year they took a trip around the world with Streeter to a remote manmade canyon buried in the mountains where barren trees looked like a graveyard. They journeyed through a weed-choked approach to an enormous stump where the grimmet tree once stood to pay homage to a good friend. To a brother. And a love. Chute would place a rose on the stump and would do so every year until they were too old to make the journey.

The vision, fulfilled.

I return to my body. Chute's standing in front of me, leans her forehead against my chin.

"I told you I wouldn't leave," I whisper.

Sadness intermingles with love. Tears run. She died long ago, but she's there with me. I close my eyes and sink into the sensation, wishing it could be real. Grateful to at least have this.

And while my eyes are closed and we're rocking each other in an embrace, I hear the ocean. It sounds like waves are breaking just beyond the grimmet tree. I slowly walk up the slab, listening to it get louder. As I approach the ledge, my mother appears next to my father. And then Spindle. Pon is there and the Commander, too. They greet me with handshakes, hugs and more tears. But as I look past the tree, it's not the Preserve I see. Everything is replaced by an ocean of people. It's like the universe came to listen to a concert, pressed together and extending out to the horizon. And when they see me, they roar. Swinging their arms, all different sizes and colors, all cheering.

"Who are they?" I ask.

"That's the universe," Streeter says. "Chute and I may be digital reproductions, but those are real people out there."

I look at my entourage. Mother and Father smile. The Commander nods. Pon looks on approvingly and Spindle's faceplate splashes with color. The tree squabbles and hundreds of grimmets look down with golden, glowing eyes. Rudder drops onto my shoulder, wraps his tail around my neck, purring against my cheek. I can feel Pivot is somewhere. I can't see him, but his presence is unmistakable. It feels like home.

"You're a legend," Streeter says. "They've been telling your story for thousands of years. They just want to say thank you."

I'm vibrating with the essence of millions of souls, like I can feel each of their thoughts, their emotions, and their presence. It streams through me like water. I thought I had no soul, that I was a duplicate. But maybe Streeter's right; maybe I became something else. Maybe not human, but something real. I understand the pain of suffering and the rise of happiness, too. I know the human experience.

247

The crowd cheers for me like they're the lucky ones to see a legend. The sound is deafening and the ground quakes. Chute hooks her finger around mine. Her pulse beats into my palm.

I want to tell them they are wrong. They're not the lucky ones.

I am.

The Legend of Socket Greeny

ABOUT THE AUTHOR

Tony Bertauski lives in Charleston, SC with his charming wife, Heather, and two great kids, Ben and Maddi. He's a teacher at Trident Technical College and a columnist for the Post and Courier. He's published textbooks, novels and short stories. You can always find out more at bertauski.com.

Made in the USA
Lexington, KY
16 November 2012